HOLYGUARD

Written by Haviti Washington

This is a work of fiction. Similarities to real people, places, or events are entirely coincidental.

HOLYGUARD: A GALAXYSTAR STORY

Written by Haviti Washington.

Suffer not the demon to live...

Five million. That's how much he has slain in his service to the Holyguard Order. Although they had technical names, the kill counters served all holyguards as devices to count the corpses to put it bluntly. Supposedly, it gave strategic information on the demons themselves in numerous ways, back to knowledge priests on Moses. Where all holyguard are created. Guardmaster Ricardo then switched on the tracking system to lock the location of the cargo that they were searching for. He looked behind to find his team ready and waiting for his command. He gripped his shield and sword, raising them into a vigilance position. The three holyguard did the same. "Holyguard, proceed forward." Guardmaster Ricardo said while walking forward in the decrypted hallways of this once glorious starship. Despite the fact there was barely a flicker of artificial light anywhere, their superhuman sight allowed them to adjust to the treacherous darkness that seemed to consume them.

But they will not falter in the line duty, nor will they hesitate when they see a mortal under the influence of demonic possession. To the best of their ability, try to save any poor soul who suffered from the Demonik. But they will annihilate anything or anyone that gets in their path. In the words of Benji's father, "If all else fails, complete eradication is the only solution." It must be done. As they walked forward into the darkness they casually noticed the wreckage that was done. Pulled wires, broken light panels, wall plating destroyed, plasma scoring riddled on both the floor and the ceiling. With some occasional electrical sparks from the busted panels they passed. Holyguard Amata smirked behind her helmet, wielding her dual axes and raising them higher. "Something amuses you, Amata?"

Through his telepathy, he spoke to her. "Nothing, Guardmaster. Just this particular hallway design reminds me of a certain starship that we had to clear a couple of years ago. The metal. The wiring.

No holographic panels. Munchkin? No. Maybe Cliverian. Maybe, a collaboration of some sort?"

Continuing to use his telepathy, he said, "You're right on both, young holyguard. I noticed the mixed design about 2 minutes ago, which means this ship wasn't created by humans, nor do I think this is an ordinary trading vessel. Which could only mean. . ."

CHAPTER 1

Aboard the Omori.

"No one thought this war would last long but then again, no one truly knew when exactly these demons entered our universe." Guardmaster Ricardo thought quietly in his quarters, for it helped ease his heavy mind during jumpspace... "From what I remember, knowledge priests of Scientia Prime, what they gathered, speculated that the demons most definitely came from a dimension or universe, beyond physical and non-physical means. Beyond mortal and immortal comprehension. Alsupra, give us guidance through these troubling times we are living in. Hmm. . ." These thoughts would race through the guardmaster from hour to hour, being a veteran holyguard and earning the prestige title "guardmaster", training his team of holyguard and a Baultus Navy captain, who without question, joined him in his near-death missions. A rare loyalty some would say.

It's been 1000 years since the birth of the Three Empires, along with a good 400 years since the formation of both the Honorguard and Holyguard Orders. Unlike the Honorguard, who were also highly skilled warriors, they served as loyal protectors for the known royalty within the Three Empires. Assigned or requested.(Emperors, their wives, cousin royalty houses, and any Xeno royalty). The Holyguard however was created with two roles in mind: Protecting such royalty figures when assigned and acting as frontline soldiers to cleanse the Demonik's presence in the Three Empires and Beyond.

"Guardmaster Ricardo, we have reached the coordinates that you have instructed Captain Zendaya to follow." His eyes slowly opened and his above-heightened senses barely was able to detect the trooper before he came into his quarters. Guardmaster Ricardo turned to see the trooper and commented. "It appears my metasense isn't the most reliable today it seems. Most concerning."

"Come again, Guardmaster Ricardo?" The trooper asked, confused. "You mean your ability to predict or foresee events before they occur?"

"To put it simply, friend, yes. It appears that as we've reached our coordinates, I've felt something ill. A great disturbance in the spiritual realm." This disturbance was so heavy for him that the very fabric of the space outside shook. "There was even a delay in detecting you before entering my quarters. This has never happened to me. Most disturbing."

"Do the younger of the Holyguard Order have or had issues with the metasense like this?"

"Yes, many of us do, actually." He replied. "Even veterans like myself would come across walls or stumbling blocks so to speak. The metasense is more burdensome than it is awarded to the impatient. For a mortal mind to hone all their senses on a universal scale, they were able to predict most attacks from enemies in battle. It took time for me but the training is excruciatingly painful, if not done right could tear the mind apart atom by atom. Although, if one has mastered this ability to the fullest, they will be untouchable to a degree. To what level they allow themselves to achieve." With one long inhale, his eyes glowed blue and with this, focusing once more, scanned half of the ship's interior with his mind. After this, a small exhale left.

We have our limits."

Both humans and Xeno, born or given these powers are more commonly known as Gifted. Guardmaster Ricardo was one of many Gifted in the Three Empires, his powers being mainly manipulation over the elements, like lightning and fire, telekinesis, and control over light itself to some degree. But most important was psionic manipulation over spiritual energy. This is something that all holyguard are trained for as the Holyguard Order fights a spiritual war as much as one that is physical.

“I see. I thank you trooper for the news you’ve brought me.” Guardmaster Ricardo raised himself from his prayer position. He was praying to Allsupra, for protection and strength for his squad and troopers who put their lives on the line, giving their all for their empires and emperors. He walked toward the soldier who spoke to him, carefully examining his face.

”Something troubling you, my lord?”

”I am informed by Captain Zendaya that you wear not your helmet while in combat engagements. Why is this?” He asked. “I don’t wear one sir, 'cause it’s a distraction in the heat of battle.” The trooper replied in a joking manner. “Interesting ideology of my own self opinion.”

They both chuckled from this small humorous moment they shared. “That’s something new I haven’t heard about.” But he can also see in the trooper's face that he has conflicting thoughts or rather a singular question that’s been bothering me for years he could see and sense.

“Is this doubt I sense in you, trooper?” Guardmaster Ricardo lifted an eyebrow and criss crossed his arms, with concern on his face.

The trooper kept his stance clean and straight, hesitant to continue. “What bothers you so heavily?”

“Permission to speak freely, guardmaster.”

A sure nod gave the trooper permission. “Why do you fight?” Silence followed.

“If it’s true that Alsupra himself is the god of all, does this mean Allsupra is also the creator of evil itself? Why has he created evil? Has this been done to test our faith in him? Our place in these dark times? For our faith in him gives us reward eternal. At least that’s what I was taught by my parents and his parents before them. But as I grew older and witnessed the horrific evils he made, we still adopt his name. Only because of our praised leader, Joshua Xanths *different* teachings.

A powerful man many consider a messiah. Even after all this, I still doubt.

Why do you fight?"

The trooper expected for him to feel angered by this *heresy*. A great sense of imposing fear or dread at the very least towards his doubtful mindset of the Alsupra religion from Guardmaster Ricardo. But to his surprise, he remained unfazed by his words and had a feeling of understanding to the trooper.

"When I lost my homeworld to the corruption of the Demonik, most of my people lost all faith in Alsupra. I remember it all. I was merely 5 when it happened. When my family, my people and the world around me slowly succumbed to evil. Even after all this, my faith remained still in Alsupra. Each day after what happened, I prayed without ceasing on one thing."

The trooper's brows lifted from this a bit, almost scared. "Which was, my lord?"

"Revenge."

10 minutes later. . .

The trooper's face showed understanding and a simple nod. "Thank you for helping me understand, guardmaster." His red shining crysamite armor gleaned from the ship's artificial lights as he bowed, having more attachments on his armor than a low-ranking trooper in the Venus Empire military and navy. The added "ornaments" that were placed or welded onto his armor showed his long years of servitude to his empire. They were a mechanical arm in place of his missing arm from the Cyborg Civil War, a Lycan skull retrofitted to replace his right pauldron, 3 medals of Unquestionable Loyalty on the left part of his chest armor, and a Trino005 advance headgear replacing the helmet for holographic HUD. That and obviously the color red signified the Venus Empire, brown for the Baultus Empire, and black for the Alvinor Empire.

"Again, thank you for helping me understand." He saluted, turned around, and left the room to the guardmaster, quiet once again. His room's energy lamps were placed in the four corners, the color being a warm soft sun glow. The blankets on his bed showed a recent disturbance of him waking up not too long ago, pillows being the same also. His desk was garnished with multiple knowledgeable books stacked upon one another symmetrically, different crysamite shards placed in order of color, and a deconstructed heavy proton pistol, battery, and all. He glanced over his shoulder to see the vast beautiful stringing colors of jumpspace. It was a sight to behold, but not to stare into for too long. He thought only of the empires he and the rest of the Holyguard Order, fighting for all these years. "Celestials be with us. For we enter once again into unknown territory and almighty Allsupra, please give us strength and protection against the unholy Demonik."

30 minutes later...

"We're approaching the wrecked B.E.T.S., Captain Zendaya." Guardmaster Ricardo said. "No sign of any living organisms on the starship so far." Cpt. Zendaya replied, her strong zumbatrian human accent having a tone of dismay. Her people, for a lack of short words, are one of the only descendants of an eastern earth that was almost lost to time.

"Hmm. It seems our ship's scanners confirm it's a B.E.T.S (Baultus Empire Trading Starship) guardmaster. I must interject though in saying how reliable is your source, eh?" She asked. "Because if it is as reliable as you say, what's stopping me from teleporting a jumpsphere right in the center of that wrecked sight of a ship?"

"No." He disagreed. Recalling a tutor that was a seasoned engineer in the field of jumpdrive technology, the words almost exact in his head. "We must not."

45 years ago...

The Recorded Words of Cheif Engineer Azmo: A Student of Ganra Archberry.

A jumpsphere is a miniaturized energy-overloaded sphere, contained within an energy shield that can contain such erratic force, that can cause massive destruction upon anything the sphere is teleported in. Jumpsheres should only be used as a last resort or a quick way to destroy a large number of enemy fleets within microseconds. As you can guess, it's meant for strictly a weapon used with just cause only.

Ah, yes. How can I forget? Jumpdrives. They have been the Three Empires main technological source of intergalactic trade and warfare for centuries. Living technology is unlike anything I've ever seen before. Jumpdrives share this passion I have for them. Without them, traversing jumpspace is impossible. Quite simply, they are like horses.

Weapon capabilities.

All impossible without the use of a jumpdrive, inside most starships that have been built underneath the reign of the Three Empires. Each drive can be programmed for numerous combat scenarios, granting the captain of the ship a vast selection of weapons and what the ship can handle. So don't go gollyknocking in thinking about creating giant cannons on the hull that serve no reason except to look *cool.* Unlimited energy, teleporting, incredibly durable energy shields that protected the ship entirely and jumpspheres.

A minor downside to using jumpspheres is that it took 30% of the ship's energy, weakening the energy shields only by a fraction.

"I know this may not be threatening at first glance "criteria" to your mindset, but the Emperor of the Baultus Empire ordered that I retrieve a package of great importance. So if the mission is successful, then yes you may carry out the jumpsphere attack." She did a slight head bow, remembering both her rank and the guardmaster. He wondered for a while, his heavy garment showed beautiful designs that only those of high stature would wear. The epaulette on the shoulders of his outfit was a synthetic golden-like alloy, made with fibers soft to the touch. The leather boots were steel-tipped and originated from the Alvinor

Empire. A humble white with blue strips carefully designed into it, with a few gold lines that surrounded certain areas of his garment.

Despite his rank as guardmaster, Ricardo never equipped his medals while on duty. Only such occasions like the great Emperor Day, to present his "collection" to the people of the Three Empires. But during combat missions, he never had them on. Her view of Guardmaster Ricardo made her in total awe. She...admired him, for some time quite often actually, she would spend time in her quarters, studying and researching his background as much as she could.

Most of the files were from the grand libraries of Scienta Prime, she swiped file after file on her personal holopad, finding very little. After 4 years of manning his holy missions, all that time, she never asked him about his "personal life". Understandable, if he doesn't want to share with the captain. After all, it's like the old earth saying that humans adored so much. "Mind your own business." Maybe she just might, but nonetheless she had a certain passion for Ricardo in such a way that might even surprise him. Not that there was too much to know about him in the first place, considering that he came to the Order of Knowledge and asked them to remove his background and history.

"Although it may seem like the correct course of action. . .I need to know the source of the demon's hiding place aboard the ship. Not only will I be able to kill them, but I could hopefully learn valuable information about the Demonik and the demons. Besides, Emperor Baultus needs that "cargo" intact and undamaged." His voice echoed in the observation deck almost museum-like aesthetic.

The ceiling is covered in 15th-century art, most of them being Russian icons. Long, pillar-like beams tall and in place, shemorite tempered glass that was in between pillar to pillar, serving as a base for the photo screens that were projected onto it. On the floor, is a singular Russian icon of an ancient knight from Earth, slaying a dragon or a demon of some sort. Since the observatory shape is circular, from the outside it looked like a globe/roundish shell. Even her ship, *the Omori*, was a Type-4 Hurricanus class starship, long and black to match deep space. Had two wing protrusions coming out at an acute angle, over 14,000 plasma cannon turrets, and was able to carry over 300,000 troopers, 400 war angels, 15,000 ground vehicles, and at least 3 Imperium walkers Type-2. . .if needed.

Luckily enough, the crew of this ship was small, only about 30 engineers, and 500 troopers, along with Captain Zendaya, Guardmaster Ricardo, and his team of holyguard. Guardmaster Ricardo spun his head to lock eyes with her. Never lost his calm, yet austerity expression the entire time. "I understand, guardmaster. I understand." Being in his presence gave her jitters every time. Her bob haircut, along with a platinum-themed coverall that was fitted with a crysamite chest armor and shoulder pauldrons, knee guards, and black leather boots that shined beautifully. Her black leather gloves, laced with a crysamite wiring, served her gloriously in the heat of battle, being able to deflect laser blasts and plasma bolts if caught in time. Once, she held the literal blade of a laser sword itself, while shooting the enemy with her Heavy proton pistol.

She is a skilled combatant and a woman of strength and faith, who remembers her place and honors it fully. But as her emerald pupils shined when gazing upon him, her 7-second trance was put to an abrupt end by a holyguard, going by the name of Benji, son of Jesse Foemasta, a former veteran guardmaster who died fighting over 1000 legions of both lower demons and demons of rank, not mention 3 leagues of cultists basterds who followed them. The one to end Jesse was a Beholder demon, said to be so powerful that, if they wanted, they could destroy entire planets within a blink of an eye. But Benji's father fought the Beholder, having no fear in his soul, and gave his life for the ensured safety of the lives of trillions if not more. His brothers and sisters in arms, the Holyguard, lost a good man that day. And his only son, Benji Foemasta, wanted to live up to his father's name and honor it with all his soul. *Suffer not the demon to live* was something every holyguard took into account. Especially for Benji.

The power armor he wore was of lower rank to Guardmaster Ricardo's power armor, similar to a Lieutenant, being already of above average build for a gifted human such as himself. Benji saluted and bowed, the formal or more traditional salute that was done now among all the Three Empires military/navy is to press their fists on their chests using their right arm, representing full devotion to their empire, respect, honor, loyalty, and passion among the ranks. "Yes, Benji. What is it?" He asked. If it was someone of higher stature/rank than Guardmaster Ricardo, a certain type of bow must be done. "The team is ready sir and waiting in the teleportation bay for boarding." Benji said. Guardmaster Ricardo nodded slowly and said, "That is good, Benji.

Very good. Tell the team I'll be down in the teleportation bay shortly after I am finished conversing with Captain Zendaya." Benji saluted and bowed once again, his helmet pocketed in his silvery red armored left arm at a 90-degree angle. He turned around and swiftly made it back to the grav lift. The sliding doors shut quickly, and Benji's figure behind the translucent metal surrounding the gravitation zoomed at such a speed it was faster than what the average organism can perceive. The observatory deck was quiet for a while, with both Guardmaster Ricardo and the captain alone together.

He sighed deeply, reaching into his garment's pocket for a small token from Benji's father. A sort of. . .promise he made to him. Facing the now starry blackness of space, with the wrecked Baultus Trading ship in view, rubbing the token in a circular motion with his thumb and forefinger. Gripping it tightly now, he faced the captain and said, "Do you think he is ready for it, Captain Zendaya? Honestly?" Captain Zendaya stared at him with a compassioning face, one who knew the promise that he kept for Benji's father. She walked closer to him and clasped his right hand and said, "You are guardmaster, sir. You must be the one to decide what's best for not only your team but also for the ones you care for. Especially. . .Benji." Slight worries were on his expression at this point. "But he's only 20 years old. To take up such a responsibility now would be too overbearing for his mind, soul, and heart as it is already. What if. . ."

She placed her left hand over his mouth gently, his squarish chin not moving a centimeter when she did this, her eyes practically shining in his view. "I mean no disrespect to silence you, sir." He acknowledged her and softly said, "None was taken." Opening his hand and slowly gazing over the token, she looked up at him once again and said. "When the time comes, as his father said, there is no stopping what his weapon will do to Benji. To change what he is. . .no. To change who he is. . .yes. So. . .giving Benji his father's weapon is completely up to you, sir. In the end, I am with whatever decision you make." She took three steps back away from him, watching him decide whether or not to give Benji the weapon. He winced his eyes, gripping the token in his hand, and fell silent.

Turning around slowly to face the Baltus Trading ship outside the observatory deck, he sighed deeply. "Captain." He said. "Yes, Guardmaster?" She replied. "Go to the teleportation bay and wait for me there, captain. I'm going to make a quick stop at my personal quarters."

CHAPTER 2

Ricardo's team.

It was quiet in the jump teleporter bay, down in the midsection of the ship, where five of Guardmaster Ricardo's team of holyguard, along with the captain herself, a team he took on almost every mission he accepted from his superiors. There were five of them, all waiting for their guardmaster and gearing up for the coming mission. Clad in Mark 9 H.G Power Armor, this is what they wore. Yes, it was the mainstay for all Holyguard who were in service to mankind. It was coated in melted durainium, thick layers of crysamite granting massive protection from damage, also giving the user of these power armors quadrupled strength and an added height of 7 feet. Not to mention increasing their speed by almost inhuman levels, impossible for the average mortal eye to track. Although being a pain to forge with, the results were worthwhile for the patient.

The alloy durainium alone can withstand any and all damage, including superheated laser swords and even high-frequency blades. High-frequency swords used an immensely high form of energy, tempered by a powerful alternating current and producing extremely high vibration frequencies, making them sharper, stronger, and lighter to carry in battle. In short, the energy blades vibrate at ridiculously high levels. "One holyguard by themself can wipe out an entire race, culture, history, planet, system within an hour or two at fearful best." An elder Knowledge priest once said to Ricardo during his teenage years. What he said is true. . .unfortunately. But that is if(And that's a very big if)any one of the glorious Three Emperors or Empresses would give such a. . .horrifying command. Holyguard is trained to be masters of combat, especially veterans being given one of the most devastating weapons mankind has ever created. A Heavenly Father Blade. A powerful, psionic energy weapon where the blade itself is formed from the mind of the holyguard, capable of cutting through even the hardest alloys the Three Empires have ever seen while creating a powerful spiritual shield that surrounds the wielder of these magnificent holy instruments of death. Adding on to what lower ranking holyguard used, those being thick durainium shields, impact hammers, high-frequency long blades, plasma axes, atomization rifles, Destroyer chainguns, Automatic plasma launchers, arm-mounted cannons, and last but not least the shoulder-mounted railgun. . .The Cleansing Shot.

Read loads upon loads of informational books, some even writing their own from battle to battle, their most sacred book being the KJV Holy Bible including the Apocrypha. In short, any holyguard is a force to be reckoned with no matter what they face. But when it came to fighting demons. . .they showed great prudence. In the jump teleporter bay was the team that Guardmaster Ricardo had during his missions. They are faithful, loyal, and honorable soldiers who served with utter diligence and respect toward their guardmaster.

Holyguard Benjamin-Coming from a family that is born-to-serve-the-Holy Guard for generations, being Guardmaster Ricardo's second in command for a few years now, Benji has led more charges into demonic hordes than any holyguard his age. That being said, he is an extremely skilled, brilliant strategist, the mainstay weapons he uses in battle are atomization rifles, his favorite being high-frequency longswords. His specialty though is quick decapitation.

Holyguard Amata- While the Holyguard had seen many halfbreeds of all sorts join for the past 500 years, the beautiful Amata outshines them all. Being half-Umari and half-Morderian, she has a powerful strain of Gifted energy, those being telepathy and telekinesis.

Weighing over 250 pounds, standing at 6'9, and a cute girlfriend to Benji. Yes, all holyguard are agile soldiers but since Amata has her Umari half, she can do acrobatic flips like none other, while also having a thick muscular body such as hers. Her favorite weapons to use in battle are the quick plasma axes, and forearm-mounted cannons. Tucked away in her arsenal also are her ancestral daggers of mysterious origin.

Holyguard Nepo-Logical, headstrong on future matters, and has a special knack for demolition entirely. Knowing nothing but destruction since the age of 8, the Holyguard Order took him in, raised him in their ways, and trained him to be a terrifying warrior. Since then, he became one of the Holyguard's most dangerous soldiers, and all demo missions were successful. He uses a long-handle impact hammer, Destroyer chainguns, explosives of his own design, and the Cleansing Shot.

Holyguard Craig-She is the medical expert of the group, having 3 years of experience on the battlefield, dressing wounds, and healing over 1789 fellow holyguard who served in the line of duty. Studying ancient arts of healing from multiple races and cultures, Craig even experiments with new but questionable ways. Choice of weaponry is the atomization rifle, forearm-mounted cannons, a short handle version of the impact hammer, and her own personal high-frequency blade, *Occam's Finish*.

They were all here, suiting up, patiently waiting for their guardmaster to come. Especially Benji, wiping his weapon he gripped tightly, having a mix of confusion and concern upon his face. While being superhuman, a holyguard strength was 3x stronger than that of a venus trooper. And an average venus trooper can already lift more than 150,000 pounds due to their rigorous workout routine and discipline. Whereas the holyguard got it easily through serums and augmentations done to the body. Meaning, when he gripped his gun, it creaked under his immense grip. "Hey, Benji. . .you all right?" Amata said, placing her armored hand on his shoulder. He blinked, looking back at her with a slight smile. She had a beauteous aura that made him calm whenever she spoke to him, something he needed during these dark times. His father was dead, never knew his *mother*, no siblings, not even close relatives. They are gone, all of them. But. . .Amata made him forget all of that for a while and even though it didn't last long, it was still mind-pleasing. The shimmering scarlet eyes, the natural gloss to her light gray skin, her soft but warm lips, and the astonishing raven-colored hair. Amata's euphonic voice is something that no man couldn't ignore for a second. Anyone saying otherwise, damn them to deep space. "I'm fine, Amata."

A slow look back to his gun, sighing. "I'm not fine." Tilting her head in deduction, Amata rubbed her thick muscular neck, raising an eyebrow. "Something with the guardmaster?" Benji nodded. "No." He replied. "Do you remember that. . . I haven't laid eyes on my father's weapon since his death?" Stepping over his left leg, quickly kneeled so she could see Benji's eyes when they were talking. "I remember. Why?" She asked, taking his hands and grasping them softly. "I always thought it was lost in battle but for the past few weeks now, I've felt it. Here, on this ship." Amata's eyes widened in shock. "You mean, your father's weapon is on this ship, Benji?" She held her voice for 3 seconds, then said.

"Strange. Strange and interesting. Being the powerful weapon that it is, I'm surprised that I didn't sense its presence earlier. Perhaps it only calls out to you." He nodded. "Perhaps. . .but it could be just my imagination." Pausing, for a moment. "You don't think that Guardmaster Ricardo-" His sentence was cut off by the immediate opening of the automatic doors revealing Guardmaster Ricardo and Captain Zendaya walking together, their faces austere as ever. The four holyguard in the jump teleportation bay snapped to a stance and saluted in the presence of their guardmaster and captain. "At ease, holyguard." Guardmaster Ricardo, his glorious silvery power armor, clipped onto the pauldrons of the armor, his magnificent cape, created to be resident to damage. Adorned with upgrades and attachments he integrated into the armor. Carrying in one arm his helm, in the other, a sword sheathed in a blue/golden glyphs-designed scabbard. Benji glanced at the weapon, but never lost his saluting stance. Guardmaster Ricardo then stopped in his tracks, while the captain kept walking towards the view screen that controlled the jump teleporter.

"Holyguard Benjamin, step forward." With four heavy steps in power armor, he was now a foot away from Guardmaster Ricardo. "Holyguard Benjamin, I believe your father interrupted me before he died that I would be the one to choose when to give you your father's sword. And I wouldn't choose any better time than now." Benji wondered why his father would say this. "Excuse my asking, but why didn't you give it to me on our earlier missions we've done together? I am more than ready to prove myself if I have to." Guardmaster Ricardo let out a soft chuckle, placed a hand on Benji's shoulder, and said. "Young Benji, I will never doubt that you are ready for this weapon." Benji raised an eyebrow. "I don't understand, Guardmaster Ricardo." Guardmaster Ricardo sighed softly."Your father, my friend, was a cryptic man in general. Always spoke in riddles and never full answers but was a good friend nonetheless. But the only partial answer he ever gave me is when he told me what would happen if his son were to wield this weapon. He said that he who wields the Sword of Moned will not only be granted power but also the infinite burdens it carries." Both Craig and Nepo murmured to each other with concerned faces, but with one quick order, they fell silent. Each of them straightened themselves. "Cease!" Guardmaster Ricardo yelled with speed, returning to his calm demeanor and stance. Sighing, Guardmaster Ricardo half smiled at Benji, slowly placing his right hand upon his shoulder and patting it in the process. "However. . .the choice is entirely up to you, young Benji. Will you take on your father's blade without hesitation, clear-minded and all-worthy? But if you think you are not ready, then you are not ready. " There was a great silence that grew around Benji, leaving everyone in the jump bay staring at him.

After Captain Zendaya was done setting the coordinates for the jump teleporter, she now raised herself in an upright position where she crossed her arms in a patient manner, tapping her boot up and down slowly and softly. "Well, it's your choice Benji." Benji, without a thought, grabbed the engraved hilt of his father's sword tightly and unsheathed it with such force that it even left Guardmaster Ricardo surprised. When the sword was fully pulled out, revealing the beautiful craftsmanship of the magnificent weapon, for some reason, its blade was imbued with a never perishing shine to it. Everyone gazed at this for some time while it was in the air, being held by Benji, his determined face showed almost as if he prepared for this moment for a long time. Benji brought the hilt of the sword slowly to chest level, turning the blade flat, and revealing his bright orange eyes. "I am ready, Guardmaster Ricardo." Guardmaster Ricardo nodded, throwing up the scabbard in his left hand, and sheathed the sword. The sound of it being covered was as if it was almost. . . mechanical. He wished he could give a full speech to him but the mission cannot be ignored any longer.

They needed to board the ship already before any other unwanted *guests* came about. He gave a nod of honor to Benji and ordered him to go back with the team. "Back to position, Benji!" He saluted, turned to the direction of his team, clipped on the scabbard to the left side of his multi-connector belt, and proceeded to the position by Amata. The two glanced at each other and turned their attention to their guardmaster. "My loyal holyguard," Guardmaster Ricardo said, tucked his helm in his left arm, and continued.

"We have purged many demons on our holy crusades across the Three Empires. From the Outer Rings of Ebun to the Sorrowing Moons of Fnir, we have purged many demons and cultists for over two decades. I know you all sense the Demonik presence on the B.E.T.S feels like nothing we ever faced before. Yes, much of the Holyguard

Order is filled with psychics, capable of sensing things unseen by regular mortals. But when an Emperor calls for our service, we must answer it. For Emperor Baultus has given us a mission of great importance, it is deemed classified until further word. By the infinite will of the Most High Alsupra, what you are about to hear, will be kept among us and us alone."

He let out a slow sigh, looked at his team with squinted eyes, and began to explain the mission. They lifted their chins, raised their arms, and saluted. "Yes, Guardmaster Ricardo! Your order shall be honored by us and us alone!" He smiled, proud of his team. "As you all know, demons seem to come in endless numbers, and the Holyguard has been the frontline soldiers who have held back their hordes for almost 4 centuries. But despite our combined efforts with the Honorguard and the vast military of the Three Empires, we have yet to find the source of where and how these demons come into our universe. But on the wrecked B.E.T.S from what information I am given, there is a cargo of some sort that can help us discover how these demons enter our universe and possibly. . . help end this war."

From this, all the young holyguard faces showed shock, dumbfoundedness, or something even in between. They have been fighting this war for all their lives, a cemented imprint in their mind knowing that any weapon of a holyguard is to be a demon's end. But to hear news of a way to end this war finally, after all this time, after all the battles their ancestors have been through, was almost unbelievable. Nepo had to speak his peace. "Something to end this war, guardmaster?" Soon followed by Craig. "By the Emperors. . ." Guardmaster Ricardo scanned his loyal holyguard, ready and waiting. "Yes, Holyguard Nepo. Something to help end this war."

Chapter 3

A meeting on Venus Prime.

The homeworld of the militaristic humans of the Venus Empire, cultured and forged in the anvils of centuries of war. Venus Prime. A mind-bending yet satisfying planet, its skies painted with a dazy red but from outside the atmosphere, is said to be so bright red, that even a thousand systems away. . .it will shine as a phenomenal eerie red star that is revered by most Xeno races as either a cosmic goddess of love and peace or warmongering god of blood. Due to the quintillions upon quintillions of these other races, cultures, histories, laws, traditions, mythos, and whatnot. Every star, from each of these specie's views or perspectives, has a different story every time. A never-ending path of mystery and history combined. Truthfully, though, the reason why it was called Venus Prime is because of the renowned Emperor of the Venus Empire, Vash Vulgrim Venus, his family name. The original name of the planet was Vi-Ahok, translated from the Lycan tongue. 8 centuries ago, the mysterious and sudden destruction of mankind's original "first" home. Earth. It's gone now, along with several other planets in Earth's solar system.

The destruction of mankind's homeworld left all humans bombarded with grief, sorrow, and pure rage, leaving mankind with a spiritual scar that would haunt all descendants for generations to come. That they will never see Earth again. Since then, the Milky Way Galaxy has been deemed "Forbidden" and "Unstable" due to more and more planets blowing up by themselves without a supposed cause. Theories from knowledge priests state that maybe it was some sort of Demonik manipulation or even some kind of prophecy that foretold the Earth's destruction but was ignored by humans at the time. Humans now, though, believe in some prophecies told by the Sacred Order of Knowledge. But today was a day of reassurance to the subjects of his empire and to discuss the ongoing war with the Demonik. Cultist groups.

The very thought of them ruined Emperor Venus's wine he was drinking in the morning before the meeting. Disgraceful and disgusting. They should be wiped clean from the universe like the filth they are he thought to himself. But, he must remember now, calm himself. The day will come. Bellum Formua, his grand palace, and home, which made up three-fourths of the city that housed trillions of loyal subjects under his rule, is truly an enormous sight to behold. Both Emperor Baultus and Emperor Alvinor, came to attend this meeting, but to also have a private talk of sorts. While the other royal officials will be discussing other means to end this putrid war already, the Emperors had a different reason to meet up. But first, they would have to greet their friends with open arms and respect. Emperor Venus was an illustrious man, renowned for his passion for war. His gaze fixed on the wind outside, comforting and peaceful. Reminds him of Earth, especially the astonishing pine trees, thrown with a medley of redwood, vineyards, and gardens. . .cherished for their multitudes of indigenous flowers from home. The smell of fresh sap slowly oozes out of small cuts made into the bark.

"Hmm. Must be Angelica." He smiled, sighed, and finally removed himself away from the 10 feet long window, jewels of red and blue outlined it. He placed an open hand on the giant, circular meeting table, where 20 chairs lay empty, softly dragging his hand across it. Shutting his eyes, cleared his throat and took another gentle sip of carefully aged wine, from his extravagant glass. "Ah, Evanglass Vines, almost 90 years old. Hmm. . .might need something a bit older." Emperor Venus said, he looked down into his glass, the wine resembling a red mirror, showing his pondering face. He squinted his eyes, examining how he barely aged after leaving Earth. Not only did barely age, but he also changed drastically. His white hair, whiter than any snow, glowed brightly in the red sun.

A few strands were across his forehead, just what he needed he would say. But his eyes. . .his eyes were the stuff of pure dreams or horrifying nightmares. They glowed bright red, almost "god-like." His pale skin was also another defining feature of his being. He shook his head, severing his gaze from the red wine. "Space life." Emperor Venus said. "Got to get used to it." He said while walking back towards a palace window, only to see 2 large Baultus Empire royal barges, slowly hovering down to the landing pads below, the booming pulsators blowing the grass that surrounded the landing pads. His focus quickly turned away from the sight when he just remembered to check if he was dressed properly and all. Usually, he would wear his military garb, spliced with beautiful silk threads that were handcrafted personally from Zericah Uman, a grosewnite, a species known for sowing anything into clothing. For Emperor Venus though, the gold was spliced with ruby. In all honesty, Venus was not a man of greed. Never in his entire existence has he ever been greedy? He just...likes the look and feel.

Even the duramale,(a sort of modern chainmail that was a skinsuit instead)underneath the main outfit, seamless to the eye. As always though, the royal mantle, revealing his family crest and chest armor he was fashioned from the finest crafters in the Three Galaxies, his cape a gift from Baultus himself, and the pitch-black boots, gloves, and pauldrons were given by Alvinor. The necklace he wore was made of some of the purest Earth metals, especially gold, and silver, from his wife, Amelia Vaughn, the empress of the Venus Empire. His glowing eyes snapped left to the sound of soft footsteps, turning in that direction. Who, in actuality, uses her gifted abilities to teleport into the room almost instantaneously. Sparks of pure energy twirled and evaporated around her. Her height was no more than 7 feet and wearing a dress ordained with star-like jewels, and a chest piece of some sort, quickly sprinted to her husband in no more than half a second flat, hugging him tightly, not letting go once. Letting out a soft exhale, rubbed her elegant face into his masculine chest and looked up at him with her emerald eyes, her pale face surrounded by her curly white hair.

In return, he hugged her tightly back, showing affection and love in the hug. He then asked, "Amelia, my love. Where're my children?". She chuckled and replied, "They're all sleeping. Including Angelica, I just got her in bed." Emperor Venus wondered, and asked her. "Tell me, did you find her out in the Pine Enclosure?" She raised an eyebrow, smiling coyly. "Yes. Cutting the bark of the trees, watching the sap slowly ooze down to the ground. But Vash. . ." Amelia's face went into a worried expression, furrowing her brow. "I worry for our daughter. What if her gift isn't a gift at all?" He raised both eyebrows in surprise and was confused. "Her beautiful wings? What would make you think her angel wings aren't isn't a gift?" She replied. "I don't know, I just-" For some reason, she stopped in mid-speech and said," Someone's coming." Her godlike senses picked up an honorguard walking down the hallway towards their location. "An honorguard to be precise." He said, with a large sigh. "It must be about the meeting. I better get going. We'll talk more about this later." She smirked with a loving inhale and exhale. "Of course, my love. Of course. You do what needs to be done."

Before walking away to the children's rooms above, she remembered. *Can't forget about that,* she would say. "Oh, your crown, my love." Vash would almost swear, but he didn't. "Damn it, you're right." He said. "Crown." He concentrated hard, imagining the object he wanted to form out of nothing. A few seconds later, a golden crown laced with the finest gems the Three Empires had to offer materialized into his stern grip. Holding it tightly, he placed the crown upon his head, closed his eyes, and took a deep breath. "Vash. . ." His wife's elegant voice, soothing to the soul. She hugged her husband ever so tightly, rubbing her head behind his back gently. "No matter what happens, our children will have a bright future. I'll always be by your side till the end of time. I will follow your decisions without question. Like my father used to say, for loyalty-" Venus, without her knowing, turned around, returned an everlasting smile and god-given hug that made her tear up and gasp. "For loyalty, trust, and respect are the foundation of any relationship. You don't have to tell me twice, because I love you with all my soul." She sniffled and hugged her tightly once again. "I know." The room fell quiet. "I know."

"My, my, my!" Lord Gilmar Victorian of the House Victoria, son of King Victor XI, exclaimed proudly at the sight of the fellow royalty that walked with him to Emperor Venus's main palace, Bellumformata, both human and xeno. Among these royalties, there was a princess, named Xingla, of the spider-like race who lived on the dark planet of Spidar Prime no bigger than Earth's moon. Their species name is Aracnidte. Made up of hollowed-out mountains that house entire megacities, cultured in the ways of the mysterious Web. The princess's *hair* was made up of 70 mini tentacles, her smooth yellowish skin gave off a certain pheromone that most others could smell. Mauve some would say. Her eyes matched that of an insectoid, while the rest of her facial and body features down to her lower leg area, looked human in appearance. With an exception of the mandible appendages on her cheeks. Lips, razor-sharp teeth, neck, arms, and even. . .***breasts***. Xingla's mandibles would click and clack along with her annoying screeching whenever her dress would get snagged by an occasional leg whenever she walked too fast. She sighed in discomfort, never barely having to wear such a conformity dress. Still, she wanted to look her best in the presence of the almighty Emperors. She noticed the young, handsome lord comment about something so loudly. "Must you speak that loud?" Her voice gurgled when she spoke." You'll be embarrassed for sure." She fixed her tentacles to a more stylish look. He laughed loudly, clearly understanding what she said. "Princess, I assure you, that the Emporers would not mind how you look at all."

"Besides, your dress is gorgeous to gaze upon!" She chuckled at his human flattery, blushing a bright pink on her cheeks. "Oh please, your flattery makes me blush. I can't stand it!" He was an eccentric one, she thought. Chittering, making up her mind if she should ask or not. She walked closer to him, patting his broad shoulder. "To be truthful, my lord. . ."

She was hesitant. "I am new to the family royalty in my homeworld, for both my father and mother have passed away recently. Both, may I remind you, were the only rulers before me and my brother. The only rulers. They have governed the Shisarx system for over 90 years, leading the people, my people, through every trial and error this universe throws at us. But, you see, I am extremely shy when it comes to conversations but at the same time. . .very curious to learn. I wish I could help out more than I usually do. Lucky for me, my older brother, King Xingar, is currently ruling to the best of his ability. And since he was too busy to come to this important meeting, he sent his little princess sister, me, to notify him of everything and anything. Please, I need your help."

She whispered gently, with a squeeze of stress in her voice." He comically raised an eyebrow, then gently grabbed her hand, held it up to his lips and placed a gentle kiss on it, and held it all so tightly. Patting her hand softly, he said. "Princess, there will be nothing better to do than assist you this hour." He did a soft bow, raising one hand in the air, and introduced himself to the radiant princess. "Lord Gilamar Victorian of the Royal House of Victoria. Son of King Victor XI and Master of War." His true height came back when he raised to lock eyes with her. "I am humbly at your service, my princess." She shivered from such a form, an elegant human too. "Finally, a human who isn't straight to politics. A good tongue you got there too." A back thought she had when admiring this human. This human man. The outfit he wore was most definitely that of a lord of human royalty. Long, sleeved overcoat, his vest rimmed with three medals of sorts. White gloves, military pants with blue lines trailing down them, black leather boots, shiny to the eye.

She grasped both of his hands tightly smiling and jittered with the multiple legs she had.

"How marvelous!" They quickly continued their walk and held each other's hands on the way their smiles outshined the Prime minister Guros of the Guromai system and even Ximas Governor of the Ximas planetary rings. Some smiled at the sight, others disapproving of them enjoying each other's company, especially human royal figures. Human royalty, mainly, not all cousin houses of the three emperors agreed with human/xeno adult relations, due to a strict "pure" human tradition, to keep the bloodline as pure as possible. The Three Emperors being the powerful men they were, didn't mind if any human had a relationship with a xeno. "Now tell me. . .Princess Xingla. . .what exactly do want to know?" She widened her eyes in surprise and asked him with insecurity. "What exactly do you know, my lord?" He chuckled, smiling with his right eyebrow raised. With a subtle whisper into her ear hole. "I am a Victorian-born human. I'm a sorta. . .natural when it comes to knowing pretty much anything."

CHAPTER 4

The wrecked B.E.T.S.

One by one, all three holyguard appeared, along with the guardmaster in front of them who appeared almost instantly by jump teleportation inside the wrecked B.E.T.S rear part, a section away from the cargo bay. The blue rings escalated and slowly disappeared from the human eye, dematerialized into nothingness, leaving the three holyguard and the guardmaster in the darkened and ruined hallways of this magnificent starship. Once lively halls are now filled with the ominous heavy tread created by the Demonik no doubt. The holyguard can only imagine what happened to the crew, but being unquestionably brave they pushed through the darkness. With a sword in one hand and shield in the other, Guardmaster Ricardo held up his wrist holo tracker showing any nearby human targets. None, besides the holyguard, were present. The next check was his HUD(Heads up display)displaying his life vitals, shield charge, weaponry he was currently wielding the moment, and lastly the kill counter.

Five million. That's how much he has slain in his service to the Holyguard Order. Although they had technical names, the kill counters served all holyguards as devices to count the corpses to put it bluntly. Supposedly, it gave strategic information on the demons themselves in numerous ways, back to knowledge priests on Moses. Where all holyguard are created. Guardmaster Ricardo then switched on the tracking system to lock the location of the cargo that they were searching for. He looked behind to find his team ready and waiting for his command. He gripped his shield and sword, raising them into a vigilance position. The three holyguard did the same. "Holyguard, proceed forward." Guardmaster Ricardo said while walking forward in the decrypted hallways of this once glorious starship. Despite the fact there was barely a flicker of artificial light anywhere, their superhuman sight allowed them to adjust to the treacherous darkness that seemed to consume them.

But they will not falter in the line duty, nor will they hesitate when they see a mortal under the influence of demonic possession. To the best of their ability, try to save any poor soul who suffered from the Demonik. But they will annihilate anything or anyone that gets in their path. In the words of Benji's father, "If all else fails, complete eradication is the only solution." It must be done. As they walked forward into the darkness they casually noticed the wreckage that was done. Pulled wires, broken light panels, wall plating destroyed, plasma scoring riddled on both the floor and the ceiling. With some occasional electrical sparks from the busted panels they passed. Holyguard Amata smirked behind her helmet, wielding her dual axes and raising them higher. "Something amuses you, Amata?"

Through his telepathy, he spoke to her. "Nothing, Guardmaster. Just this particular hallway design reminds me of a certain starship that we had to clear a couple of years ago. The metal. The wiring. No holographic panels. Munchkin? No. Maybe Cliverian. Maybe, a collaboration of some sort?"

Continuing to use his telepathy, he said, "You're right on both, young holyguard. I noticed the mixed design about 2 minutes ago, which means this ship wasn't created by humans, nor do I think this is an ordinary trading vessel. Which could only mean. . ."

"I detect movement, sir!" All the holyguard snapped their heads when they heard Benji shout. "Behind and in front of us." Guardmaster Ricardo also sensed the incoming threat, he readied himself with his shield and sword in hand, then gave out a command with his low, void shaking voice. "Holyguard, kill position." They primed their long-range and twirled their melee fiercely when this order was given out. Back to back, Guardmaster Ricardo took the front, Craig on his left, Amata back to back with Benji(unsheathing the Sword of Moned), and Nepo took the rear. They raised their weapons, blades beaming brightly in the darkness, the light from the blade reflecting off the armor, making the silvery armor they wore. . .almost star-like. "Ready thyself, holyguard!".

Guardmaster Ricardo stood tall and proud, full of honor, wisdom, valor, and most importantly. . .faith. Not just in himself, but in his team. Rampaging footsteps approached faster and closer. Guardmaster Ricardo raised his head, his psychic presence booming with power. "Holyguard, show no fear to thy enemy! Let them taste the unending wrath of Allsupra's might. Bring peace to the possessed and suffer not the demon to live!"

Amata's plasma axes hummed loudly when she gripped them fiercely. Her eyes glowing with rage, just begging for combat to come to her out of the shadowed hallway. "From the deepest darkest realms to the endless plains of Gamorta, we stand to watch for the Demonik's unholy presence in our universe. And by the Celestials, those who convert to their wicked ways, I shall destroy them! By the Emperors, your existence will be no more in this universe!" Amata raised her axes into kill position and shouted, "For the Emperors!" In one voice, all holyguard afterward shouted the same thing. "FOR THE EMPERORS!!!"

Out of the darkness, 10 to 15 Demonik cultists sprinting and screeching came from both directions of the hallway. They wore black armor, covered in sharp spikes from head to toe. The armor itself was a sort of way to show how devoted they were to their hideous beliefs. The sharp extensions inside the armor would pierce into the body, causing them unending agony, feeding the malevolent evil that they served more and more. The helmet they wore covered everything except their grotesque, outstretched mouths. Filled with razor-sharp teeth, drooling a black acidic ooze, their stench smell of rotting corpses.

An ordinary human or Xeno would immediately vomit just at the sight of this unholy abomination. Luckily for the Holyguard, they aren't regular humans anymore. One of them cursed in Demonik language, then shouted at Guardmaster Ricardo. "Mindless dogs of the Emperors, you will never leave this ship alive! The package belongs to Delmia!"

It cackled, and his unnerving voice echoed. They grew closer. . .and closer. . .and closer. . .CLASH!!! A sword against an unholy sword, the holyguards sliced, chopped, and decapitated the incoming Demonik cultists that either leaped, rammed, or slammed themselves against some of the holyguard's powerful psychic shields that surrounded their bodies. Also, having a thick durainium shield was a superb addition to smashing, bashing, and slicing if needed. Horrific, yet always slightly comical to Amata when some of them became mush when they met her mighty fists, chuckling from such dark amusement.

She resumed her righteous slaughter upon these. . .Demonik puppets. She hated every single one of them and used her axes to tear apart any of the Demonik scum that stood in her path. Amata dodged a flaming Warhammer of dark, purple fire that created a poisonous shockwave when it reached its target, capable of killing any mortal in an instant. But alas, holyguards aren't mere mortals. Caught it just in time, she pulled so hard that the arms of the cultist ripped violently off, letting out an ear-piercing scream that could shatter sumeron glass without trouble.

With a quick movement of the hand, she dropped the hammer and mustered enough strength to headbutt the damnable thing, sending it flying across the dark hallway, passing Nepo, Craig, and Benji. She could hear bones and armor breaking as it made contact with the floor. She gave a soft but grimacing smile. Praise the Emperors that the Holyguards were fast enough to dodge the sharp jagged blades of the cultists, for the swords they wielded were unnatural in origin. Granted, Gardmaster Ricardo, along with his team, has slain many lower-ranked demons, cultists, and horrific abominations, for some years now, once in a while, an entire swarm of higher-ranking demons.

Even a Smograr General. But when it came to fighting minions of the Demonik Realm, every battle they fought was not to be taken lightly at all. Even when fighting something as low level as these Demonik cultists. For when they conformed to the ways of the Demonik, they gave up their truth, righteousness, and innocence for a promise of wondrous gifts given to them by the Demonik Gods. These gifts were the strength of entire multitudes, faster than the fastest speeder made, and were functionally immortal unless killed by weapons wielded by someone of Gifted background. For instance, one of the very few beings who were capable of killing demons instantly was Joshua Xanths, hated by all demons most dearly, revered by those who follow his ways without question and respected by his friends. Long live Joshua Xanths! Bam! Bam! Bam! Craig unleashed her anger upon the cultists, firing more than 25 shells from her pistol, each exiting the short barrel, completely and utterly blasting them apart limb from limb. One came from behind, attempting to swing a crude Demonik ax straight down with a forward chop, covered in black unholy symbols.

“These weapons aren’t even capable of cracking our psychic shields.” Craig scoffed. “Even so, it’s best to still support everyone’s shields.” Her Gifted ability was that of supporting or increasing the power of one’s Gift without straining or being in great pain. Craig casually stood her ground, without a worry on her face when the ax came down upon her shield, shattering instantly into a million pieces. It staggered the cultist so much that he fell to the ground, his back on the floor, looking up at the imposing slayer of demons. He said, “HOW?!?! I was sure that it would-”

His words came to a bloody end when she shot her last shell into the target’s chest. Causing him to become a mere black smudge on the floor. "Demonik scum.” Since she was in the middle, she acted as covering fire for fellow holyguards. Except for Guardmaster Ricardo, who was on a 360-degree killing spree all over him. His energy shield wasn't even touched yet. Showing even more how skilled he was in melee combat, not to mention how he used his cape. But by the Celestials, his cape was made from crysamite thin threads, leaving his back completely protected from all attacks from behind.

As for the others, an occasional crackle from the cultist's weapons, being deflected from Benji's dual sword attacks. An HG high-frequency longsword on his left, with his father's weapon, the sword of Moned. Interestingly enough, Benji felt nothing of the blade when he wielded or even used it, leaving him pondering in combat what the sword's potential was. From what he can remember, tales from other older holyguard who fought alongside his father, are up for debate. But then again, holyguard can never lie to each other, so, therefore, making the stories of what his father did in battle true? Then again, many holyguard disliked his father's *mysterious* methods he would use. Benji blocked three attacks with Moned, then quickly pushed with unforgiving might, sending them rolling and tumbling down on the floor. Since these cultists were much smaller than Benji, he could look down on the Demonik puppets and say, "DIE FILTH!!!"

Tightening his grip on both swords, loosened his neck, stretched his shoulders, and sprinted forward with thundering footsteps. Before they could even react, he did a frontal somersault, then with both swords. . .SLASH!!! While landing back on his feet, three heads dropped from their parted torsos, two with agape mouths and one with his teeth barred. The thud of each head was an assurance to Benji's ears, smiling from the new *kills* he acquired. From his view, Holyguard Nepo had already obliterated 6 of the damn cultists, each becoming goo piles strewn across the hallway floor and ceiling, within no more than 2.5 seconds. In the hands of a trooper, the Cleanser can be a cumbersome weapon to carry in the heat of battle if not trained for it. But in the hands of trained holyguard, especially Nepo. . .the shoulder cannon can be used in close-quarters combat before the automatic overheat system kicks in, faster than a proton shotgun.

One of the cultists was armed with a plasma chaingun aimed directly at Nepo, pulling the trigger, clotting blood squirting from its overgrown teeth, and laughing hysterically. Large violet projectiles, capable of melting through 800mm of thick armor easily, more than 340,000 bolts came impacting upon Nepo's psychic shield, each bouncing off and dissipating into nothingness. Feeling a splash of energy in his head, Benji turned to find his gaze locked on a 23-year-old engineer just 5 feet away from him, who came from behind, leaning on the wall to her right, with a pained expression.

"By the Celestials!" She grunted, a hand on her head, the other wielding a plasma ax, and was crying now. Both her hair and her Baultus naval coverall were stained with blood but it wasn't her own from what he sensed. "My head!!" She said while falling into the arms of Benji, dropping the ax. Had pale skin that matched that of the regular Venus Prime human, her eyes were bloodshot, tears streaming down her cheeks. "Help me!"

"My lady." As she dropped into his armored arms, his vision flashed red and his body fell cold. An unholy entity inside her. "By Alsupra! Craig, this officer has a defiler demon in her! Prepare your trauma kit."

Benji honed his senses to pinpoint where the deep seeded evil was, only to realize...

Painfully wincing with every move she tried to make, she mustered enough strength to place her hand on his wide chest plate, uttering four weak words. "How bad... is it?" Behind the helm's chrome-colored visor, a face of assurance and pure faith in Alsupra that this young woman will be fine.

"The defiler..." He paused. "Has rooted itself to your soul too deeply at this point, where if I attempted a psychic rip..."

"What?" She asked weakly.

“I cannot lie.” Benji said. “Your soul will be torn apart alongside the demon itself. You won't survive the process. Your physical condition, the multiple outcomes, is the same. But need not worry. By Alsupra's might, I will destroy the demon that dwells inside you. For there is another way. . .

It's a cruel method. I'll put you under a coma like state, so you don't have to endure the pain. You will survive. This I can give. I'm sorry.”

Shame. Although it was a flickering feeling for Benji, shame was enough to cause his blood to boil.

“It's okay.” A smile formed: one out of comfort and not of fear. One of trust And understanding. “Do it. If I die, at least I die knowing that my faith pushed past the impossible. Please, just do it quickly. For I am frightened.”

"Forgive me.” He uttered.

He looked back, flashing plasma fire and clashing of blades happening. Roars and bloody screams of his fellow holyguard could be heard from both sides of the long hallway. “Grenade!” Amata shouted. A large explosion followed.

He outstretched his hand, a small pulse of electricity swirling in a circular motion. In his palm, it was no bigger than a disc.

"Wait.” She gently pushed him. “What is your name?”

"Milady. . .” He struggled. “I can't.”

"Please.” A single bloody tear came down her face.

“Benji. My name is-“ From behind, throned black tentacles latched out for his limbed and fiercely squeezed exposed neck, wrapping it completely. “Wha-“ They appeared to of the ships walls, like maggots breaking from a corpses. “Ack! No!” His movement was cut off, the tentacles could feel the strength of his pulling and pulling. “Rrargh! No.”

"You will watch.” A crackling voice echoed in his mind. “You will be a witness. Watch. As she serves a greater faith than that of Alsupra. Watch. As she becomes a glorious power among you insignificant mortals." With a forceful jolt, the tentacles made his direction towards the young lady on the floor. Who in her pain, looked back at him with fear. "Watch."

"NO!"

"Ack! Benji." She began, trying to stand. "I'm sorry." But with a sharp pain in her heart, she let out an agonizing scream, with a horrendous Demonik voice behind it. She couldn't control herself at this point, for the defiler had already taken over most of her body, trying to forcefully get out to face Benji and kill him. To prove itself for its Demonik Gods. A painful wave shot through her body like a solid projectile, causing her to double over, her knees becoming jelly as her small hands shot to her stomach area. "Forgive me, Benji." She could barely make out words at this point. "Please, forgive me."

"NO!"

Controlling the utter rage he felt at this demon who dared use an innocent young lady as its host. If he could strike it down now, he would. But he can't, for the defiler hasn't revealed its true self to him, therefore, he cannot kill it. If he were to strike, it would most certainly kill her also, he knew. "She will survive." He thought internally, her screams present around him. "After it reveals itself in the physical realm, I can kill it. Please, Alsupra. If there's going to be one innocent life I must save today, please let it be her. I beg you, lord of all things good."

In this traumatizing event, he could only watch her suffer at the hands of this foul demon.

The voice chuckled. "WATCH."

Another powerful surge of Demonik energy flowed through her, fleetingly losing control of her body, and stumbled in the process. Out of instinct, her hands shot out to prepare herself for the hard fall, veins engorged, tinted nearly with a glowing red. Even though it was meaningless, she tried to fight back the transformation, no matter how futile it was. The defiler was morphing her body against her will, turning her into a. . .demon.

She screamed in agony as the sound of her bones cracked, grew and shattered from the intense mass and mutations. The floor below her gave in by the continuous weight, her fists tightening and even crushing what metal alloy was in her hands.

Her back arched as her torso began to grow, stretching her clothing past its very limits. Her new body tore through the fabric of the tank top she wore underneath with ease, shedding the ocean-blue coverings over her arms, chest, and back. Engulfed in agonizing pain, a single word could not describe what she was feeling at this moment. The young engineer, her body now top heavy as her upper frame expanded and took one last look at Holyguard Benji. Lost among a vast array of negative emotions streaming through her head, she struggled to stand on her feet.

Trying to find her footing, her growing feet struggled to find balance in her constricting boots. Bursting through her footwear as her coverall leggings grew tightly against the rapid mutatiling growth happening to her body. Gushes of blood spilled out of her stomach, intestines conforming to like armor wrappings around her body. Nearly transformed, she stumbled over to the wall on her right, jolting her arms out to brace herself.

Feeling the raw power from the demon that was inside her, her left hand, without effort, went through the metal wall. Trying to focus, attempting to pull her hand out, sharp painful gushes came from her forehead, she dropped to the floor and felt what they were. Horns. Short, bloody demon-like horns.

"Benji." She said wearily, as brown hair grew longer and longer until it covered half of her wide back. The pain grew and so did she, bulking beyond the normal limits of a regular being, she screamed. Until she fell silent.

Motionless. As if a whole other being had entered. Benji could sense it and it made him feel weak. With a cruel ease of their tightened wrap, the black tentacles finally released. Benji weakly kneeled to the floor, his breath shuddering with anger..

The defiler is here. Slowly, as she rose from the floor, her thick muscular neck bulged from the horrific transformation that took place. Reaching 8 feet in height, the coverall was ripped and torn, revealing more of her body, pulsating veins growing and growing. It was no longer her, it was the defiler that had control now.

"My, my, my, my!" The defiler exclaimed rambunctiously, balling her fists and raising them into the air, laughing hysterically at her human body.

Muscles bulged and pulsated as she outstretched herself, yawning when she did so. Her mouth was filled with a new array of razor sharp teeth, especially her four long canines, viscous-looking and a snake-like tongue long enough to wrap around a person's neck entirely. Even rubbing behind her neck and even hearing a loud pop.

"DEFILER!!" Benji shouted.

"You." The defiler smiled, slowly leaning her head in his direction, her eyes glowing red and hungry. "I know your name. Oh, Benji, forgive me!" Chuckling, her twisted comment left her blackened lips. "Save me, Benji! Save me!"

"CEASE YOUR CRUEL VOICE!" His grips tightened.

"To be honest, I didn't expect her to put up a righteous fight like that. She is a righteous one, one that believes that her faith is stronger than my powers!" Placing a foot in his direction, he tightened his grip on both his swords, ready for her to attack.

The defiler allowed its black saliva to drip down her chest, tongue dangling also. Then she said, "The hardest ones though are the best to taste. Ya know, I have an unfathomable taste for human meat. So sweet, so juicy. Especially the righteous ones. They taste the best. Fortunately, your flesh would have to do."

As the defiler grabbed the ax off the floor, it changed in design instantly, becoming something from the realm of Demonik could only come up with. It was cold to the touch, ordained with miniature metal faces warped and screaming, covering the handle. And the head of the weapon, the ax head, no longer produced plasma but a look of jagged-shaped metal and crude material.

Examining the familiar weapon, she pointed it at the holyguard, saying. "Let's see how you taste, okay?" In a moment, the demon vanished from his sight. Where did she go? He kept his battle stance still, waiting for her. . . "Surprise!" Came the defilers' voice from behind. His psychic senses warned him of the incoming danger, he had to react fast.

More importantly. . . either block or dodge fast enough. Incredibly fast too, if he wanted to dodge the defiler's light-breaking attacks, for one vital hit on his body would mean an instantaneous death for the young holyguard. This was a split-second decision. Block or dodge? Dodge or block? Dodge. . . "Celestial be with me." Benji said, then quickly decided to dodge right before the powerful swing of the defiler's large Demonik battle ax, morphed from its original weapon that she once held. The large battle ax halfway into the floor, she growled in annoyance, struggling to wrench the killing tool back into the fight. Now that the defiler is open to attack, he can finally expel the demon from her body.

Filled with anticipation, then charged in with a full cleaving swing, both the high-frequency sword and the Sword of Moned were imbued with holy energy, blinding and bright. "By Allsupra's light, your existence will be no more, defiler demon!" He roared, continuing the strike, until he heard a wet sound of flesh tearing, glancing to his left he saw a large long pink, meaty tail around her rear area. Its appearance was that of a skinless tail, purple veins, and bony spikes and all. It was long enough to take out 4 and a half men with one swipe, having enough force behind it to break most if not all the bones of the body.

. .with ease. Swinging her tail so fast, it stopped him in his attack, hard enough to put him 3 feet into the wall.

CHAPTER 5

Heal thyself, holyguard.

His vision flashes white and blurred from the sudden impact, due to her tail directly hitting him on the face part of his helm. He felt like a piece of fleck. Every bone in his body felt completely broken, though his suit's healing systems quickly activated at the first sign of pain. His vision started to clear up for a bit, hearing his fellow holyguard faintly in the background, out of his view, finishing off the last of those Demonik followers. "Ben!" Amata screamed.

He can hear Amata yelling in a charging manner as she was targeting the defiler. The sound of her plasma axes humming, spinning, and swirling, aura with a powerful telekinetic boost. Holy against unholy. Hearing the conflict continue, hearing Nepo and Craig join the fight, but where was Guardmaster Ricardo? He couldn't even hear his voice, nor could he feel his almighty presence. "Ughh!!" Benjamin tried to move from the cramped position he was in but groaned in pain in doing so. An alert message popped up on his visor, showing how much damage had been done to him. A two-second hum prolonged, until a human-like voice said, "Major spinal fractures located in both the lower and middle vertebrae."

He sighed, in frustration, knowing full well where this is gonna end. "I already healed all your fractured bones in your body but your spine-" He tightened his fist in preparation, cutting off the female voice. "Do it." There was a five-second silence."Fix my back, Serma." He groaned, gritting his teeth. A loud beep sound within his helm chirped. "Command confirmed." A three-second timer popped up on his visor.

He squinted his eyes. . .3. . .2. . .1. . .SNAP!!! His eyes widened in shock, gasping for air, then sighed in relief. He regained himself by making sure all his motor functions were working, hands, arms, legs, and all.

He rotated his neck, then said to Serma, "How long was I here Serma?" With a quick reply, she answered. "35 seconds, sir." He immediately launched himself out of the crude position and landed back on his feet. He was back in the hallway where he was fighting a moment ago. He turned to his right, seeing Holyguard Nepo in a vigorous neck lock with the towering defiler, Amata being choked out by an unforgiving grip. And Craig, Craig was coiled on the floor with a Demonik battle ax, halfway in her chest armor.

From what his helm scanners confirmed, the ax was somewhere between her breasts, sliced through her ribcage, and barely touching her heart. Sighing, she was fine. No need to worry about that right now, but what he did need to worry about was that damn demon!!! Using one of his Gifted abilities, he summoned the Sword of Moned to his grip, the very blade itself glowed with a warm, blue aura that surrounded it, and the entire atmosphere of the hall boomed with the sound of this mysterious weapon. His armored gloves clinked and he lunged forward hard! Once again, he shouted, anger shaking in his voice. "By Alsupra's light, your existence will be no more, Defiler demon!" He moved so fast, that another one of his Gifted abilities kicked in, making him almost as fast as light itself and. . .SPLOSH!!!!

Right through her chest out the back, black blood and all. Her eyes shot open with surprise and with a heavy thud, collapsed slowly to her knees. Her glowing eyes grew brighter and brighter as the defiler demon inside her died, an astral form of it came out enraged and volatile. With her mouth fully outstretched beyond human levels, she passed out from pure mental(not to mention physical) trauma and exhaustion, Nepo ungripped the lock hold he had on her, grabbing her large wide shoulders, spiky bone protrusions, stopping her before she could fall. Both Nepo and Benji breathed slowly from this, then Benji asked, both exhausted. "Are you alright, my friend?"

With a slow nod, Nepo looked to Amata, who was coughing after escaping the loosened grip the defiler had on her. Nepo ran to Craig who was still on the floor, wrenching out the battle ax from her armor. "You all right, Amata?" Benji pulled the sword from the young woman's chest, quickly placed a hand on Amata's shoulder, and knelt to her level. Gasping for air(whatever air was left on this forsaken carrier)through her helmet's multi-filter system, capable of converting most toxic gasses, chemicals, viruses, or even water if needed, to save, breathable oxygen. She placed her hand upon the throat area of her armor, rubbing it with severe irritation. "What took you so long?" Amata said, a slight smile forming.

"Broken bones." He replied, sheathing the Sword of Moned, then helped raise her to her feet. Nodding in thanks, placing her left hand on her hip and scanning the floor for the axes. Looking left and right, she just about had enough of searching for the old-fashioned way, raised her arms, and opened her fists in a grasping position. A loud, magnetic hum boomed throughout the hallway. Glancing to her left, to see two corpses move violently when the Umari made plasma axes unsheathed out of their soulless corpses.

They came to Amata's two hands, coming at a speed so fast that she had to catch them simultaneously. Sighing, Amata had made 3000 *creative* kills with these weapons so far, cleansing a planet in no less than a single day. Still, nothing could compare to her ancestral weapon, the Sajat Eorgos, she hid away somewhere. Sajat Eorgos, meaning All evil fears it in the first Umari tongue, sent a cold shiver down Amata's backside.

"Benji. . ." She asked, his attention now turned to her. "Is she alright?" In an already kneeling position, he stretched out a hand, using another of his Gifted abilities to see if her soul was still untouched by that Demonik filth. Thankfully, in a matter of seconds, her body slowly morphed back into a human form, eyes closed, with her slumberous face. Beyond tired. . .definitely. "She's fine." From his utility belt, he pulled an instant blanket, contained in a metallic cylinder, shot out, and covered her completely. "Serma, scan and confirm."

He commanded, and two beeps sounded. "Physical damage: 15%. Mental damage: 19%. She will survive, sir." Serma said. They both sighed in relief. "Alsupra be praised," Benji said, but then he remembered. . .how could he forget! "Amata, where's Guardmaster Ricardo?" With remembrance on her face, she looked forward and replied, "A dimensional rip appeared out of nowhere..." Balling her fists in anger she paused. "Demons, demons pulled him in faster than I could blink. Blast!!! I should of—" An abrupt screeching came from the shadowy darkness that grew and grew. They felt Demonik presence closing in on them, attempting to put fear into their minds.

But alas, in the great words of Joshua Xanths, fear not the demon! For the forces of the Demonik fed off negative energies, emotions, and beliefs that were throughout the Three Galaxies and Beyond, granting them an endless supply of negative energy to feed off from. They readied themselves for what may come. Whispers, whispers of corruption, and demon voices were in their head.

How dare they, they thought. Their psychic shields glowed brightly as the voices grew louder and louder. "Nepo, pick up Craig, now!!!" He shouted the order to him quicker than an ignition of a high-frequency sword. Nepo reacted accordingly and slouched Craig over his right shoulder. The power armor they wore added to the impressive strength they already had as augmented warriors of Alsupra. Without the power armor, they matched entire platoons of venus troopers.

Holyguard Benji, without hesitation, took swift action, and went down to the young woman, placing his arms under her knees and around her back. Holding her close to him and him alone. Back to back, all the holyguard wield their weapons high and vigilante, except

Benji. He focused on amplifying their psychic shields, surrounding even the sleeping engineer.

They waited for anything to appear out of the darkness, for demons were unpredictable like always. "Stay strong, fellow holyguard." Benjamin commanded. "Stay strong!" Smiling underneath her helm, Amata raised the ax heads, the heating plasma humming louder and louder with every gradual elevation with them.

They hummed loudly now, echoing with spiritual energy, glowing blue with a hue of green over them, crackling and sparking. Nepo's cleanser cannon was primed, glowing brightly from the compacted plasma, through the cooling vents that covered the barrel.

Within moments, more of the whispers grew louder and faster. Until actual figures materialized in the dark shadows that threatened to consume them. From what they can make out, their skin tone was unnaturally white, lengthy, skinny arms that reached down to the floor, dragging them carelessly.

The humongous claws they had, scrapping them across the floor, hissing at them in a taunting position, some even laughing wickedly. For what seemed like 40 to 45 seconds of corrupted eyes watching, a voice broke out of the incomprehensible language that the demons grumbled to each other.

It was a ragged version of understandable english. "Your bodies. . .will. . .serve. . .as. . .perfect vessels for us. . .once. . .well. . .of course, your souls have left completely. We would rather not have an annoying host when we take control." It snickered, revealing its disgusting yellow, sharp, jagged teeth. "So please, accept our offers, mortals. Please. . .be ready to die."

He drooled grotesquely, with no eyes that they could perceive and it slowly, creepily lifted its arm, hand open, pointing directly at Benji. He felt disgusted, with what he saw in front of him, actually even dared to speak such unholy words to them.

"Throughout my servitude to the Three Empires, no cultist or demon dare speak such words to me or my fellow holyguard. . ." Pausing, he observed closely how this abomination appeared. "Judging by your twisted horns, the engraved spirals into your putrid flesh, the tucked fleshy wings. . .demon of rank, no doubt." They screeched, a bloody howl, black-hearted smiles, their claws digging into their chest, black acidic blood squirted out, hugging themselves most inhumanly.

"Yes, we have, in a way, been watching you for some time now and we must say, you put on a good fight. Without a doubt, you'll never reach the cargo alive, nor take her off the ship. She's too important to us." Behind the visor, his eyes widened. "Her?" He asked forcefully. The demon closed its mouth, grinning widely in excitement. "Ohhh. . .I said that, didn't I?" His sarcastic tone annoyed Benji deeply. "It doesn't matter. . .none of you will be alive in a very, very, short while."

It began to laugh, laughing so hard that all the others joined in the laugh like a cascading waterfall. "SILENCE! Your demonic words mean nothing to the Holyguard of the Three Empires, you filth!" All three holyguard girded themselves for battle. "We will cleanse your presence in our universe and the Demonik will know true fear!!" Amata and Nepo both agreed in applause.

"Death to the Demonik!" Both shouted. The demons frisked their claws, preparing themselves to attack, making a gurgling laugh.

"Then you die, now! Here and. . .NOW!" In one fluid motion, all the demons launched themselves forward to the holyguard, screeching and roaring, then a sudden huge, bright orb outshined the entire hallway, revealing who created this beautiful light. He had a blue aura, blinding to the eye but felt warm to the soul.

They watched in awe as they were in his presence, but were familiar with this awesome power. "Guardmaster Ricardo!" Amata shouted with praise, humor, and joy in her voice.

His power armor was nearly wrecked beyond repair, the Heavenly Father hilt he wielded was broken, almost fractured, psychic energy flowing through the cracks, dripping and burning a light blue. His helmet was missing, blood was trailing down his forehead, showing his head was severely damaged.

Despite this injury, he showed no pain in his face. Enraged, his gifted energy formed a small yet barely visible halo, surrounding his head. Teeth gritting, he spoke. "My young holyguard, keep together. Stay strong in Alsupra faith! Stay strong!" His voice implored, inspiring, and invigorating! The demons all huddled around each other, with great fear of the empowering guardmaster.

"You. . .you should be dead!!! Dead! Dead!" His eyes locked contact with the demon who uttereth anything from his abominable mouth. "Is that fear, I sense, demon?" With a fluid motion, he raised the hilt to his chest, forming the psychic blade, closing his eyes, and said, "Please, Alsupra. Give me the power to vanquish these demons from the universe. For your everlasting power, gives all who believe in you, true strength!"

The demons viciously growled in torment, just hearing words of his holy stature. "Say nor more, human. Your words annoy us!" The lead demon crouched into a hostile pose, swerving its head back and forth like a snake.

The demon's mouth drew wide, wider than any human can make, and shouted in its Demonik tongue, a battle cry of some sort. "Be ready to die, Holyguard!!" Roaring, they charged at the holyguard with such erratic and unnatural movements, moving at speeds so fast, the ordinary eye could barely see.

With his helmet's faster-than-light racking system, combined with their spiritual and physical training, the holyguard could target them easily. Guardmaster Ricardo scoffed in disgust, a loud booming sound of uncontrolled energy grew louder and louder by the second. Soon, a small energy orb formed inside his palm. All his fingers were in a semi-claw position. He quickly looked to his team, shouting a single command, loud and proud. "Hit the deck!"

CHAPTER 6

The pondering captain.

From her command chair, Captain Zendaya sat quietly, pondering the mission at hand. Pondering about Guardmaster Ricardo and the team. Pondering about. . .what was the *special* cargo? Her head was filled with questions, not enough to frustrate her, but just enough to make her almost worry.

Fingers interlocked with each other, posed in a brooding type of state, pointing finger rubbing her ball-shaped chin and sighing deeply. But like a gentle breeze, she shut her eyes, drifting off in distant memories of her past. Mainly her childhood. Zendaya could picture it clearly like it happened yesterday.

Wondrous beaches of blue sand, the glistening waves receded calmly, a cool breeze and cloudy sky, the sun peeking through with curiosity. Distant towering spires far from shore stood, shooting beams of blue light into space.

Shield generators, enough to cover a continent and having multiple of them built across the planet, could shield it entirely. As a small child, Bloomshore Cove was a beautiful place to visit, especially with her family. "Hey, Zen!" A low, gruff voice called out to her. "Time to go home!" With a turn, Zendaya looked upon her father, Visad Blanchet, a scarred naval captain of the Baultus Empire.

Along with her mother, Lady Moria Blanchet, Keeper of Winton-5. Both of them smiling, he opened his arms in an embrace as his excited daughter ran to him, giggling when doing so. Rubbing her cute face in his lavishing shirt, his purple trench coat flapping in the breeze. She looked at him and said,

"Father, will I be just like you, when I grow up, father?" Chuckling, he looked at his wife and wrapped his left arm around her. "My daughter, you will be more than I have ever been. Believe that, and you will go far in life." Stroking her hair back, placing a blue flower. "Alright, Zen?" A nod without hesitation, holding the hands of both her parents.

Walking back onto the path to their little beach house, the memory disappeared into black as her tired eyes opened. "Father. . .mother. . ." She whispered. Beep beep. The command console sensors beeps rapidly, indicating another ship nearby. Her eyes shot open, immediately locking her sight on the sensor.

A small hologram appeared in the middle of the console, about 3 inches high, revealing a miniature model of the spaceship that was near. The computer systems scanned it as a Hormik Battleship, heavy arrangements. The scan continued, showing lifeforms aboard this 14 miler, all shrouded with Demonik readings. The scan finally confirmed that the ship was filled with humans, pure humans. "Cultists scum" She scoffed loudly, the light from the hologram showed on her face.

"All humans too, how disgraceful. Weak basterds. No doubt they were all power-hungry morons and depressed souls, easily manipulated by the Demonik's trickery due to their loss in Allsupra's faith." Tensed up in anger, slowly knowing to control her emotions, then calmed herself.

Her mind took swift action, tapping numerous hologram keys on the curved commands console that encircled her. The buttons she pressed were weapons priming, activating defense systems, engaging the stealth field(rendered the outside of the ship invisible.), and increasing image.

The sight of the cultist ship came into view when she pressed the last one. From what her screen showed, the once Hormik Battleship was set ablaze completely. Well, the rear part of the ship that is, probably because it still used a Sling-engine or Zemeton engine.

Both still needed fuel and yearly maintenance, repairing if needed. How it remained on fire, especially in space, was as mysterious as the hordes of the Demonik. The Sling-engine model is a human-created engine that dates back to Ancient Earth's ingenious designs, capable of taking any H2O as compatible fuel.

The Zemeton engine is of newly built design, utilizing environment-friendly biofuel created by Omnobuild, put into safe civilian-related vehicles, such as hovercars, hovertrams, commercial flight space crafts, etc.

However, none of these engines could match the capabilities of the jumpdrives, a magnificent creation of humans and the Celestials. While their recognition spanned beyond the Three Empires, their influence and intellect were unquestionable.

Captain Zendaya remarked on the quick history lesson within her mind, remembering the now and putting off then, a dreading gaze combined with a disgusted expression, she pressed three keys to activate three primary weapons.

"Plasma turrets, Slugshot cannons, and Konami cannons all online, captain."

Being in service to the good captain far longer than a veteran trooper, the ship's computerized voice sounded that of a middle-aged man, who replied to her formally and strictly. His name is Calis and he is a guardian program, sentient and living. . .in a way. "

Scanning target. A hormik battleship, corrupted by the Demonik, most definitely. I recommend a more stealthy tactic than your usual methods, captain." Her eyes locked to the console below her, where Calis formulated a mini battle plan that involved staying behind stray bits of the wrecked B.E.T.S. as a form of clever cover, while also being in stealth mode.

Those eyes of hers glistened from the hologram keypad that illuminated her elegant face. Her brow furrowed.

“Why?” A smirk formed. “You don’t like my style, Calis? You're scared I’ll get us killed or better yet . . .you?” Even though she couldn’t see Calis’s face, she knew for a fact that he had a displeasing expression.

Annoyed, even. “It’s not that I dislike your father’s style, It’s because I rather not have to repair your ship constantly after every naval or planetary battle we have.” Leaning back on her command chair, she wondered. “Exhausted?” She asked.

With a swift reply, Calis replied. “I am a guardian program. Incapable of being exhausted, Zen. You know this better than anyone.” Slowly raising herself, Zendaya gripped the arms of her chair and said.

“I do not doubt that my ship can more than handle a puny hormik battleship, taken over by idiotic cultists who believe in Alsupra know what. Oh, turn off the stealth field while you are at it.” Calis sighed.

“As you wish, captain.” From what the Holyguard Order gathered from multiple battle reports, combined with vast military of the Three Empires, fighting these cultists and locating their sanctuaries on different worlds, it is clear truth that these cultists have sacrificial altars in honor of either one of many of the Demonik Gods they worshiped.

“Blasphemy.” She thought. So far, 7 “all-powerful” gods exist, granting their hungry followers access to unholy miracles, the stuff of nightmares.

Their powers are so terrible, they can wipe out all life on an entire planet in seconds. Of course, these were mere rumors based upon multiple accounts and stories from individuals who have witnessed these horrific feats performed supposedly.

Nonetheless, they are enemies of the Three Empires. Her ship's sudden movement caused her to jerk back slightly, and the three accelerators forwarded her into a collision course with the hormik battleship.

Assumingly, the enemy starship was slow, and could barely turn in time to react to any quick attacks from left or right, giving Captain Zendaya the upper hand in this attack.

The tactic she was using is used by many fleet destroyer captains in the Baultus Empire, her father mainly. Because in the Baultus Empire, many of the ships(including the small ones) were built with an incredibly strong stern, constructed to dish out ramming attacks and come out with very minimal damage to the ship. Captain Zendaya braced herself for impact.

Their reaction to her oncoming attack, they fired proton torpedoes, plasma cannons and even fired a single slugshot round. The 50-foot-long slug thankfully grazed the energy shields just slightly.

Creating what humans call shield breakers, capable of inflicting tremendous damage if not instantaneously ignoring the energy shields depending on how the slugshot round is manufactured.

Without the help of at least one slugshot round, it would take the continuous fire of at best 1 million plasma turrets or 50,000 proton torpedoes for more than 1 hour on a certain area of the ship just to deplete the shields .

And that's if the ship is staying still, moving very slowly, or is internally compromised. Although she did feel the two torpedoes that hit the stern and portside.

She glanced down at the shield bar, monitoring them at the same time. "Shields is at 97% combat capacity. Still good." The hormik continued its defensive fire as much as it can, but it didn't halt the powerful momentum her ship gained over time. Was very close now. . .very close.

Sweat trickled down her forehead in anticipation. "Impact is imminent," Calis roared. "in seven, six, five, four," Captain Zendaya gripped the armrests with preparation. ". . .three, two, one!"

Emperor Venus, more than a man most would say, might as well be the physical manifestation of war itself. After the Celestials gifted the

Three Emperors(along with their loved ones), they changed physically, mentally, and spiritually. Despite their godlike appearances, the emperors and empresses still derived from human origin. But after all their experiences in the Three Galaxies so far, whether they were still human was up for debate.

But being called for a war meeting, especially by the emperors themselves, was already troubling to the mind. Emperor Venus was troubled so much that he would arrange a secret meeting of sorts with both Emperor Baultus and Emperor Alvinor.

Was it about the different Demonik cults that were forming like unwanted weeds in an illustrious garden? Perhaps it was about border disputes with warring planets who declared independence from the Three Empires? Or maybe. . . about their children? Whatever the reason, it was very important(or maybe even urgent) enough for all the high-ranking military officials to be called.

Spidar Prime, being one of the largest planets in the entire Venus Empire, had a population of 346 trillion, with a military count of 77 billion(15 million in reserve) and a navy of 800,000 battleships. Long before the Three Empires came, the Aracnidtes created their means of space travel 200 years before humans created the first motorcar. Some xenos amusingly would even say "the plow".

But that might be pushing it to the levels of a deep insult to humans, so it's best not to mention it at any time. Xingla carefully entered through the palace doors without breaking intricately designed floors.

Her four insectoid legs were uncannily sharp to the touch, trying to the best of her ability not to snag on the dress she wore. Combined with the fact that she rarely wore a formal dress and the fact that she got extremely nervous when surrounded by a large crowd of royal figures, she wasn't taking it very well at all.

Thankfully though, the kind Lord Gilmar, was here to assist her today. The honorguards she passed remained motionless, holding their plasma staffs in their right arm, while propping the durainium shields below their chest.

The interesting thing is that honor guards or the Honorguard Order started first before the Holyguard Order. While Emperor Baultus created the Honorguard program after his attempted assassination on one of the blue moons of Eveon Prime, a planet where political scandals between two races occurred constantly: The Cermites and the Xlon-furtite.

Known for their planet-destroying tech and sophisticated minds. The Holyguard, on the other hand, was created by the religious fanatic Joshua Xanths. Joshua Xanths is a man of religious background, on Ancient Earth he was a feared general, respected by all who followed his beliefs.

His skin was that of burnished brass, beaming pupils of psionic energy that cracked out of his eyelids. Standing taller than most Lycan, wearing magnificent golden durainium armor, followed by a large white cape, designed with astral drawings of stars, buckled onto the massive pauldrons.

Not much is known about his past, but it is said that the Emporers knew him as a close friend of the emperors and knew him as a close friend on Ancient Earth.

Friendly or not, that didn't change the fact that most xenos didn't agree with the beliefs he shared with the rest of the Three Galaxies and Beyond. One of the first races he tried to integrate this ideology too was the Aracnidtes. They. . .were partially insulted by the god he was trying to introduce.

So, yes. . .the Aracnidtes and the Holyguard Order(particularly Joshua Xanths), didn't get along well with each other. But unlike the rest of her people, being the youngest female adult of their race, she sought ways countlessly to create a stable peace between the Holyguard Order and her people.

If it was even possible that is, of course. But. . .it was still unknown to her or anyone else what this meeting that Emperor Venus assembled. Especially the presence of the other two Emperors unless it was something very urgent. Especially Emperor Venus, being the strongest one of them all in terms of strength.

Something must've troubled him dearly to call a meeting. "Almost forgot," Xingla exclaimed. Her vision faced the left where Lord Gilmar was, smiling gently and posture, unlazy. "Lord Gilmar," She paused. "If you can be so kind, can please introduce these other high officials to me, please?"

The white pupils of her black eyes shined, and a couple of squeaky cute chirps from her mandibles clicked and clacked. "Nothing would please me more, Princess Xingla." The right arm of Lord Gilmar wrapped around her in a slow and kind approach, somewhere halfway between her lower neck area.

Pulling her against him, they continued their walk as he began to speak. "First off, the gentlemen in front of us, the frog heads. . .High General Phori and military Ambassador Pilk of Amphibo, a backwater planet in the Baultus Empire. There's also Governess Muta, their race was in charge of many of the trade routes in the Baultus Empire, some even saying they look identical to cattle from Earth. Being dubbed humanoid bipedal cows or *minotaurs*. Not surprising, considering that Emperor Baultus himself is also here at this meeting, titled as urgent no doubt. And from what you told me, you are here on behalf of your prince brother, because he was-how should I say it-too busy with homely matters?"

Yes, of course, he was right! But actually, she did come because her brother told her and something else. A coded message. . . "Come to think of it, I just received a message from one of the High Generals in the Venus Empire, requesting my presence here. I don't tend to wonder too much until I am given more on the matter."

Lord Gilmar chuckled, then glanced behind him. He whispered into her ear hole and said. "Well, probably because of Planet Aorick and what happened there."

Pausing, knowing full well that the information he was about to share is top secret. But, he trusts her because she's(in his standards) a beautiful xeno woman and honest to heart. He continued. "Judging by our presence here, along with either one or three individuals from one of the Royal Houses of Baultus or Venus.

Mixed in the group we have some xeno royalty included amongst them, yourself included." With a slightly confused look, she blinked. "Oh but don't think I am racist when it comes to xeno's. Unlike some humans, I respect all races. No matter the religion, belief, culture, etc."

She smiled. "But please, my lord, backtrack or else we might trail off into religion or history. I hate when I trail off-topic. Makes my thorax sore and my tentacles twitch. So please, tell me. . .what happened on that planet you mentioned earlier? Hmm. . .yes. Aorick. Planet Aorick." Lord Gilamr's face switched back into remembrance.

"Oh yes! Right. Umm. . .to dumb it all down in a quick understandable fashion, easy to remember to the point where even a child can remember it. Both royalty and important military officials from across the Three Empires are here for the meeting. Not all, but some. The meeting is gonna be about Aorick and what happened there. Which was truly horrifying."

Shocked eyes sparked from Xingla. "Horrifying? How?" She asked, turning her head in a side glance. "Truly horrifying as in the entire population of the planet, converted and transformed into Demonik abominations. The local militia in the world didn't even last a couple of minutes. If the rumored reports are correct. . .these demons were far from the ordinary types that both the troopers and Holyguard have to fight. And what's worse. . .it was a farm world." A soft gasp escaped her. "How many. . .were on the planet, Lord Gilmar?"

Her voice quivered in fretful fear. Pausing, the young lord needed to compel himself. "36 million lives lost." Shaking her head in doubt at his words. Could it be true? Could she believe them? These rumors? Could she? "This can't be true, Lord Gilmar, right I mean. . .36 million lives?"

The worrisome eyes of the princess were more noticeable now to the young lord. He grasped her hands firmly, but with care. "I learned these stories from my older siblings who govern nearby star systems near that planet. Even so, Emperor Venus, alongside the other emperors, could have called this meeting for a completely different reason, other than what I just said."

Both of their hands held onto each other as they walked down the flowery-designed hallways of Bellaforma, each step they took left an echo among echoes.

The ten individuals (Lord Gilamar and Princess Xingla included), found themselves in the grand meeting room of Emperor Venus's palace. It is the Chamber of Vorwick, having all their attention turned towards the unflinching ever present gazes of The Three Emperors.

CHAPTER 7

Demons.

Zraamm!! Huge bolts of energy, pure psionic energy, amassed the entire hallway and ceiling, the walls ricocheting the massive energy that he charged, directing its holy light before those wretched demons attacked the young holyguard. The young holyguard fell to the floor, purposely, so that they could dodge the Guardmaster's oblivious attack.

They watched in awe, their heads following the movement of the bouncing bolts, creating a singular energy beam, powerful enough to completely erase both the demon's physical and spiritual presence in the universe, sending them screaming and dissipating in their astral forms back to the Demonik Realm. Painful enough to torment them dearly, it also nullified their return for a short period.

Roughly 2 minutes or less. The face of Guardmaster Ricardo, stricken with pain, blood streaming down his forehead, his seething anger dwindling, lowering his badly damaged arm to rest.

He panted and panted from both the psychic overload he experienced and expelled. His eyes winced from the crisped, charred armor surrounding his badly burnt right arm.

Examining it, he gripped the hilt of the Heavenly Father's blade and sighed softly. Fourth-degree burns, with several arteries bleeding. Some of the melted durainium, mixed with his blood, dripped down onto the floor.

Only temperatures that reached close to the levels of a large sun, were able to bring a stable melting point towards the nigh-indestructible alloy. His power armor's healing system activated and was still intact. . .thankfully. The sound of the automatic painkillers, mixed with a cooling mist spray, covered the arm completely.

Finally, a minor surgical process was to fix his shattered wrist bones, and a healing serum was directly injected into his lower forearm area. Sighing slowly, watching his once damaged arm, steadily healing burnt skin and muscle tissue within seconds.

He opened and clenched his fist, testing if at least all the nerves were still intact. "Minor damage." He commented. Multiple footsteps from his team's approach grew louder and louder.

Guardmaster Ricardo turned to find Holyguard Benjamin, carrying in his arms a young engineer, directly in front of him, with Amata guarding his rear. Nepo, along with Craig finally conscious resting her left arm on his shoulders. They looked upon their guardmaster with careful eyes, Benji was the first to speak.

"That energy. . .the power. . .it was like my father's technique. The Blue Enflame." Guardmaster Ricardo nodded in agreement. "Your father shared his knowledge of how to master this power. Unfortunately, like a young novice, I have a long way to go before mastering something your father created from his Gifted abilities. Especially the Blue Enflame."

Guardmaster Ricardo's head swerved to his left in the direction of where the cargo hold was. "Right now, we must hurry to the cargo hold immediately. Those demons I vanquished moments ago will return with an entire horde to fill this ship within minutes."

Turning around, facing the now lightened hallways that were once consumed by darkness, showing a clear path to the cargo hold bay. A sudden dread showered on all the holyguard present in the hallway, all of them sensing powerful Demonik energy forming nearby.

"Run, holyguard! We must run!" Faster than a microsecond, they bolted towards the sliding door that led to the cargo bay, Guardmaster

Ricardo leading the charge. As they were running, Craig glanced back behind their tracks, and due to the battle she had with the Defiler demon, her battle helm was gone.

She didn't have enough time to regain her lost piece of armor. "Kraisar!!" She swore beneath her voice. Returning her focus towards the front, her long flowing silvery hair, followed her head movement. Orange eyes, tiny lips, and a round nose. Embarrassing, she murmured to herself.

Being this a Baultus Empire Trading Ship, most likely three years old due to the designation code it had: B.E.T.S 15.03. The hallways that were built in these gigantic spaceships were over 10 feet in walking space and 9 feet in height. Having the capacity to hold forty million crew, while the cargo capacity was triple that.

Meaning the hallways were created in such a way that they somewhat matched the maze-like tunnels of Galmorp. The hallway that the holyguard was in though, was one of the straight ones.

Leading Directly to the cargo hold, having at least a thousand feet left between them, which they could reach in 30 seconds easily. But the sound of immense Demonik screeches and roaring grew loud behind them, only pushing the holyguard even faster.

The door was nearing closer and closer, Nepo and Amata glanced at the new threat that gave chase to them, moving with supernatural speeds, and unnatural bodily movement alongside the foreboding darkness they carried with them.

Holyguard Craig just recalled that the metal sliding door was shut, her increased vision allowed her to see it was in lockdown mode. Her eyes widened, shouting to her guardmaster. "Forgive my words, Guardmaster Ricardo but. . . but what about the door?!" With a side look and a loud and joyous laugh, he said. "Prepare yourself, young Craig."

The armored arms of the guardmaster went into a ramming position. "Holyguard Amata!! Be ready to collapse to ceiling us once I break down the door!" Ammata took the order without question. "Yes, Guardmaster Ricardo!"

Craig once again took a glance behind them, only to find compiled upon compiled bodies mended together, their black acidic saliva splattered everywhere, with each crawling hand, scraping the floor beneath them.

Their glowing, fiery eyes, dripping tears that sizzled their skin. Itching to dig their teeth into the holyguards flesh and rip them apart from limb to limb.

This is a Demonik Horde or at least a small portion of it. Just the mere presence of a Demonik Horde sent shivers down all the young holyguard. Guardmaster Ricardo was ten seconds away from the door.

Now it is five. . .four. . .three. . .two. . .one! RAAAAPAM!!! In an instant, the door came flying at speed, destroying cargo containers that were in the way, nearly pushing them seventeen feet in all directions. Scraping sounds from all the holyguard halt in their speed with their arms to the floor.

Guardmaster Ricardo, being the one leading the front, almost made contact with one of the pillars, using it to halt his movement, while turning to face the exposed doorway that revealed the dark hallway.

Demons crawling on each other, hungry for the blood of the holyguard, thirsting for it. A hideous mixture of screaming, laughter, and crying, which in turn created an unholy presence, voices piled on voices from the Demonik beyond.

Being the skilled melee user she is, Amata did a full-body jump twirl, launching herself into the air, and slicing the entire section of the hallway ceiling, causing it to collapse. The Umari steel plasma axes she used easily cut through the interior of the ship like melted butter.

That's saying plenty, considering that most ship's interiors are made of astrosteel, a common metal that resists high-frequency blasts, which ranks higher above plasma and laser technology.

Slashing nearly 25 times to the ceiling area, bringing down wrecked metal beams and wiring, crashing down onto the demons extremely. As she did this, Amata did a backflip, just in time to dodge a demon who leaped quickly forward and scratched her visor just barely.

She gasped in surprise, landing on a kneeling position and waiting to see if the newly made barrier could hold them. She waited patiently and calmly. Nothing but silence. Amata arose, sheathed her plasma axes, and turned to her left, where she found Craig checking the wound she sustained on her chest.

She could still see the area the Demonik weapon once was and said. "How's your chest, Craig?" Craig smiled, a reassuring smile that she always did when she knew everything was okay.

"I'll be fine, Amata. . . Don't worry." Holyguard Craig walked towards their guardmaster and said. "Guardmaster Ricardo, permission to examine your injuries and check your power armor's healing system is still functional."

Without a single word, he slowly nodded, confirming for her to proceed with her checkup. Craig first checked his head for any fractures. From her scanner, there were a total of 2 fractures. The power he wore was damaged almost beyond repair after being pulled into the dimensional rip by those demons.

But. . .as always, he was fine. Due to the numerous surgeries, implants, serums, or what some holyguard call blessings granted to them by the messianic figure Joshua Xanths and his loyal knowledge priest that studied the art of bioaugmentation. Even the H.G. power armor was created by the intelligent minds of Joshua and Ganra.

The head priest, Genre Archberry, known to some as a heretical knowledge priest, was marked zealot by the Sacred Order of Knowledge, for following the ways of Joshua Xanths.

Even she follows him because she fell madly in love with him the first time she saw his enormous power demonstrated firsthand. Built in with an automatic healing system and a guardian program, capable of repairing even the most devastating blows a normal being couldn't survive.

That being said, it didn't mean they could be careless all the time when in battle, especially someone of Guardmaster Ricardo's stature. If his power armor is badly damaged though, plus the multiple injuries, there could be only one explanation for how he's like this.

"A Demonik General, bloodlust, full of rage, and nigh unkillable." He said. "After being pulled into that Rip, I fought it for some time but I'm all right, though."

Nodding, Holyguard Craig opened the medical kit she attached to her belt, grabbed a medium-sized syringe, filled with a purple liquid, and inserted it into a vein she could find on his neck. Patching up wounds this great is an easy task for Craig but she still had to remove a couple of metal fragments that were on the side of his forehead.

He let out a soft wince of pain. "Sorry, guardmaster." Craig apologized. Pressing three buttons on her wrist gauntlet, chirping sounds from it revealed the guardmaster's power armor diagnostics and damage report. From what she was seeing, 67% of the armor was unresponsive, healing systems were at 80% efficacy, all showing signs of gradual depletion and his heart rate was 40 beats a minute, which is normal.

"This isn't good, guardmaster. Your vitals are showing gradual depletion, sir. Internal bleeding in the lower chest area, 14 fractured bones, your vision is blurred, not to mention a slightly fractured jaw, and your right arm has been burnt to a crisp, covered by only painkillers and the healing spray. You are suffering from the pain, sir. Dearly."

She sighed, looking around her, sensing her fellow teammates having signs of weariness in them. Unable to bring herself what to say to him, she looked up to her commanding officer. "Without your helm, guardmaster, your strength level in battle will be only at the half. If not, drastically lower than that. Praise Alsupra that were in the cargo hold because if what I sense is true to my spirit, that means that our cargo is. . ."

With a slow pat on her pauldron, Guardmaster Ricardo nodded in agreement. "Near." He said. "But it will take more than some demons and minor injuries to stop a guardmaster of the Holyguard Order from completing the task he was granted by one of the Three Emperors. We will continue on and so will I. Do not care for my condition, young holyguard. For the pain of the body truly never lasts forever, for we fight not just a physical battle but also a spiritual one against powers who wish to corrupt the light of our universe. For our souls burn brighter than any sun and purer than a flawless stargem! We will find the cargo and complete our mission, no matter the cost. Press on and suffer not the demon to live!"

Turning to the seemingly endless rows of cargo upon cargo, he smiled and gripped his Heavenly Father's blade, focusing his psychic energy to form the blade itself.

Craig got up from her kneeling position, clipped on her medical kit, and placed a hand on his crisped arm. "If that is what you wish. . ." Craig said.

"Then we will follow you without question." Guardmaster Ricardo sensed positive energies burst into the damp and cold atmosphere that surrounded them, and looked back to find his team all standing upright, spirits charged with loyalty and devotion not just to the cause, not just for the Three Empires, but for him.

Holyguard Benji, who still carried the unconscious young engineer, walked to his guardmaster and said."Without question." Followed by both Nepo and Amata, raising their weapons against their chest simultaneously.

"Without question!" They roared. For more than 57 years of service to the Holyguard Order, he has never felt this much devotion to him in his entire life. Smiling, Guardmaster Ricardo knew that this mission would succeed, regardless of any higher powers who wished to halt them in their path to completing it.

They will succeed.

Without warning, the entire ship abruptly shifted, causing everyone to momentarily be unbalanced, while still standing and preparing themselves for danger. Except for Guardmaster Ricardo, who stood his ground, and looked to the ceiling of the ship, using his telepathy to find out what just happened.

"What is this?! Are the demons manipulating the ship itself?!" Nepo questioned, then carefully listened, outside the hull of this B.E.T.S.

"No, this is different. It sounds like plasma shelling or-" With respectfulness, Guardmaster Ricardo finished his line. "Cannon fire from a hormik battleship, overruled with 2 million cultists or more. They're trying to board this ship again and Captain Zendaya isn't going to allow that to happen. She will defend this ship as long as she can, but from what I can sense more cultist ships are approaching. She will buy us enough time to search for the special cargo but that is it! So everyone, prepare yourselves!" In unison, they replied to their guardmaster.

"Yes, guardmaster!" With a swift nod, he once again took the front point and ordered Nepo to pass a spare automatic proton scattergun he holstered just in case, loaded with 5000 shots with an extra 2500.

Nepo threw it to him, knowing full well that his guardmaster would catch it. Catching with his right arm, gripping the handle tightly, and checking the battery power on the scattergun's huge barrel. It was fully green.

Weighing more than 20 pounds and could be fired at a ridiculous speed, he turned to face Holyguard Benji, alongside Craig, who was carefully injecting a pain killer into a vein she could find.

He could see Benji's face distraught for this poor innocent, who had suffered at the hands of a defiler demon. "This should ease her pain,

Benji. I can use my powers to heal her, but not here. When we're safe, I'll do what I can. Alright, Benji?"

Sighing, he replied to her. "Thanks, Craig." Closing his eyes, seething with anger. "I could only watch her suffer, Craig. Her body grew to levels beyond human limits. Bones, muscle, and skin all transformed."

She must've felt so much pain. And I could only watch." A quick silence fell on him.

"There was nothing you could do, the defiler demon had already taken hold of her body. Even if you did strike the defiler at that very moment, you would have killed her in the process. You made the right choice, Benji. You made the right choice."

Feeling great comfort from her honeyed words, a small soft smile formed on his face. "Thank you, Craig." Hearing four heavy footsteps approach them, both Benji and Craig found themselves in the gaze of their guardmaster, saying.

"How is she, Craig?" He asked. "She's fine, sir. I will be able to do more once we get back on Zendaya's ship."

Using his Heavenly Father's blade as a brace for himself, he placed a gentle armored hand on her forehead and inhaled deeply.

So much pain she has felt, so much grief upon this weary soul, sensing all these specific raised emotions, Guardmaster Ricardo uttered three words to her. "You poor girl." He said, then sighed.

"Holyguard Benji, I know you better than you know yourself that you will protect this girl with your life." Both he and Benji smiled at each other in agreement. "Good. Protect her well."

Horrific screechings and menacing laughter from what sounded like more of those cultists, echoed as they ran past the multiple containers stacked to almost 16 feet, the holyguard readied themselves for combat.

Seeing Benji carry her carefully with his arm, Guardmaster Ricardo took both weapons he held and shouted. “Suffer not the demon to live!”

CHAPTER 8

Battle outside the B.E.T.S.

Created by Shinzou Konami during the Cyborg Civil War, the Konami cannons are one of many devastating weapons mounted on most Baultus Empire Astro Navy ships. Alongside multiple obscure ones to include, making their use in battle extremely versatile and deadly, firing large purple translucent energy spheres(having a diameter of 7.2 miles)when combined with the shield-breaking Slugshot cannons of the Venus Empire Astro Navy, gave superb results.

What gave the Konami cannons their special place in the vast arsenal of the Baultus Empire's military was its shield-disabling capability, the momentary shutdown of most energy systems, and rarely, instantaneous destruction of all electronic devices on board the targeted ship. Making the effects of these powerful weapons somewhat random, they served their killing purpose no less. This was exactly why Zendaya, at all times, to the best of her ability, stayed clear of the hormik's Konami cannons. If more than four hit the energy shields of the Omori, the damage would be so catastrophic that she would have to forcefully retreat to wrecked B.E.T.S parts to maintain cover from the enemy.

But due to the ramming speed attack, she commenced just now, the cultist hormik didn't get a chance to fire their Konami cannons. The impact was so great that it caused a massive shockwave throughout their entire ship, different levels of it started exploding because of this. Most of the frontal part of the Omori energy shields were affected by it, only taking minimal damage, but sliced a top portion of the ship off, where the bridge/command deck was.

Through her command console screen, she could see how much damage she had made. Letting out an explosive laugh, Captain Zendaya shouted. "Direct hit!! Ha, ha, ha!" Quick with her fingers, she pressed 25 buttons that targeted the hormik battleship, activating more than a dozen plasma turrets to rain fire. "Calis, direct full power to the turrets I activated, now!"

His holographic mini-body appeared once again at the center of her command console and said. "Yes, captain!" In mere seconds, the turrets of the barrels pulsated with overcharged plasma, growing louder and louder until they were fired. Laser tech has always been known for range than plasma, which has far more penetration power, but fails to reach targets at great distances.

So, instead of using regular plasma, Baultus Empire starships use something called concentrated or potent plasma. Potent plasma is far more effective because it keeps its devastating piercing power, while also being capable of firing long distances repeatedly. In quick succession, a booming sound came from each turret, firing large green projectiles down on the hormik battleship, exploding in no less than five seconds, sending a massive shockwave that moved the Omori slightly, after it exploded.

The life reading on her command console went flat after this, meaning there were no survivors at all. Sighing, she pressed one button on her keyboard to target the wrecked B.E.T.S, scanning if they were still alive, and, to her comfort, they were fine. "Captain," Calis said. "I'm picking multiple slingspace ruptures, portside, portside!" On the screen in front of her, flashed multiple targets that headed straight for the location.

An alert noise came blaring as one of the cultist ships fired a two Slugshot round, the first exploding on contact with the Omori's energy shields, obliterating them. The second was a direct hit to the stern area of the Hurricanus Class ship. One of the propulsion engines was down, this wasn't good, she needed to give back a swift reaction to this attack and she had to do it now, or else a third Slugshot round would most certainly damage the Omori to the point where she couldn't move the ship at all.

They must be reloading because usually slugshots take a while to reload and prime. Her mind raced through different scenarios, deciding which should be the best course of action to take. "No better time than now, captain!" Calis shouted. "Shut it Lemme think. Calis, activate the propulsion engines and put them on full power!" Not doubting whatever plan she cooked up in that organic brain of hers, he followed the order and activated the propulsion engines to full power. Captain Zendaya then pressed a small holoscreen, enlarging it to view the multiple propulsion engine's angle/direction.

Pressing onto one of them and turning it to a 90 degrees angle, accelerating the Omori upward so fast, that another Slugshot round whizzed past and just barely scratched the hull. "Calis, full power to all plasma turrets!" Swiping tabs away on the holoscreen with haste, Captain Zendaya pressed the plasma turret's control and aimed downward once again at the new cultist battleships beneath her. With roaring hatred, she shouted gloriously. "RAIN FIRE!!!"

FOR ABOUT 15 MINUTES the meeting continued and already the Three Emperors had shared the recent updates with the rest of the royal figures who came, along with many high military officials. These were rumors that had been confirmed across the Baultus Empire for some time, Emperor Baultus the most distraught looking of all of them by this.

These updates were about matters such as planetary defense, trade routes under Demonik control, independent planets going quiet for months on end, billions injured or dead from the war, and the recent horrific attack on the farm world Aorick. Numerous murmurs, shouts, and arguments flew across the circular meeting table where royalty and high military officials debated on how they needed to access the situations at hand and the saddening ordeal that happened on Aorick. The Three Emperors, however, remained silent and merely watched the ongoing arguments happen, sitting in their large luxurious gravity thrones shining magnificently, golden and color coordinated.

Red, brown, and black. One of the many sources of divine transport for the Three Emperors, they would use these for formal meetings usually, especially today. For it was going to be a long meeting unless said so otherwise by one of the Three Emperors. Sitting there with big eyes, Princess Xingla chirped and also watched the many arguments being thrown left and right. Across from her seat sat Lord Gilmar, who had his clenched gloved hands in a raised position, thinking up a way to stop these arguments quickly and fast.

Feeling cute eyes watching him, he snapped his head to Princess Xingla and smiled, raising one of his pointing fingers to her in an acknowledging gesture. Letting her know that he's trying to come up with something. He noticed her tentacles twitching from all this commotion. "Multiple worlds have been falling to Demonik control like flies to rotting corpses! And Aorick?! Aorick's defenses were weak, we all know that!" A Morderian general shouted, his voice similar to that of a falsetto opera singer. "But that was their fault, my emperors!" Feeling offended, one of the royal figures rose up from his chair and said."Blasphemy! Forgive me, my emperors but the Bolter family will not take responsibility for Aorick! We just can't! Just because a planet's military force was significantly lowered due to our emergency enlisting program, doesn't mean we should take the blame!"

He scanned the table, pointing at a Lycan war chief who was in charge of managing that sector where Aorick is. "If anything, the Lycan Clans are to blame, my emperors! They were in charge of safeguarding that sector from the unholy demons!" A soft growl could be heard throughout the room, as the Lycan war chief barred, revealing a powerful set of teeth. She was wise though and remained in her seat for the time being.

Being almost 9 ft to 10 ft tall in height, a middle-aged Lycan like her was still considered young in her culture and traditions. She was 194 years old. "I would choose your next words wisely, you human brat." Her diplophonic, breathy voice boomed, and her snout barely opened, making it almost seem like she didn't even move her lips at all. "May I remind you that some of my loyal warriors were posted on the world at the time when the demons attacked? Sadly, they didn't survive but. . .by the time I got word of what happened, there was nothing I could do. Everyone on the planet, they all were dead way before me and my warriors could react!"

A scoff left the lips of the Bolter family member, turning his head in disbelief, raising the war chief's anger tenfold when he did this. Just before deciding to get up from her chair and declare battle on the Bolter family member, Emperor Venus roared a command so loud that it stopped her dead in her tracks, perking up her ears and making everyone who was present fall silent instantly.

Everything in the room shook when he did this, although the honorguards who stood vigilantly moved not an inch somehow. "Enough!" Emperor Venus commanded. "I will have order in my empire, especially in my house and especially in this meeting room."

Letting out a deep sigh, he continued. "To put your worrisome minds to ease, we as the Three Emperors, along with knowledge priests and the supportive help of the Holyguard Order, have worked ceaselessly to discover how the demons managed to attack Aorick without them knowing. Unfortunately, the answer is grim." Out of everyone present, Lord Gilmar spoke first. "Grim, how, my emperor?"

Emperor Venus looked to Emperor Baultus, who had already an answer ready for a while. "We know for a fact that the Demonik Realm feeds off powerful negative energies, by spreading their fearful horrendous beliefs, seeding mass hysteria, and inflicting great pain upon the innocent masses of the Three Empires and Beyond. But demons from the Demonik Realm cannot enter our universe by regular means, meaning that they could only view our universe as is, but for some reason, they can never interact with it fully." The Lycan warchief tilted her head, confused and astounded by the seemingly intelligent minds of the Three Emperors. In everyone else's eyes, their great intellect matched that of the Celestials. To others, they were more than gods.

"What do you mean *fully interacting*, Emperor Baultus?" A Galomite's grand general asked politely, his floppy ears were in the way of his vision a bit. Even though she was only 97 years old, coming from a race that basically could theoretically live for hundreds of years on end, her knowledge of the Demonik was very small, like an adolescent child.

Having fluorescent purple skin, black eyes, and glowing purple pupils, her chest armor was adorned with medals, each obtained by prestigious acts of valor and honor she achieved in a thousand battles.

"They could only appear to us as phantasms or whispers, voices, planting heinous thoughts in our minds. Weak-minded and grieving individuals are considered as easy prey to demons. But it doesn't stop there. These are some of the methods they enjoy. They can also resurrect corpses to do their bidding and possess masses at will, but this rarely happens due to them still barely managing to fully interact with our universe. A weak string line, if you may. Unless . . .they form Rips."

A moment of silence stayed in the air, cold and unnerving. "Rips, my emperor?" Princess Xingla asked. Out of his shadowy silence, Emperor Alvinor, dark and mysterious, spoke to her. His gravity throne positioned in between the other emperors, moved forward slowly as he commanded it to do.

"Rips or demon portals are means of multidimensional travel, giving them control to do almost anything they please. Creating doorways that lead from our universe to theirs. The Demonik Realm. And from what my scout's reported, searching on the planet Aorick for days now, my suspicions have been confirmed. That the planet Aorick was attacked by demons utilizing a Rip, without anyone on the planet during the time knowing. A coordinated attack."

Alvinor continued, raising his fingers together and clasping them together. "In theory, demons have been using portals they call Rips to attack planetary systems unnoticed and conquer them within a single day if not less." Shocked faces and covered mouths scattered across the table, some leaning back on their chair with anger in their eyes. The Morderian general clenched his robotic fist and respectfully asked the mysterious Emperor Alvinor.

"Forgive me emperor, but what do you mean by these portals? These Rips? Are you saying that the demons are using teleportation similar to that of jumpspace technology? Are they using jumpspace to teleport now? Is there nothing touched by the Demonik?" Immediately Emperor Baultus broke into the conversation, his attention locked on the worried general.

"Heavens no, my good man! Demons from the Demonik Realm have not even attempted to touch jumpspace, hell, I even channeled jumpspace energy directly into demons on multiple occasions! Completely vaporized from the universe itself!"

Stroking his scruff beard that he attempted to grow for some time now, went into a more relaxed posture on his gravity throne and pointed sternly at him. "For your comfort, the Demonik Realm has no interest at all in jumpspace. But they do have an interest in this universe and we are trying to solve why. So far what we know, demons have been creating Rips on numerous worlds in both the Baultus and Venus empires. Amassing millions upon millions of cultic followers, with each growing minute! But fear not, my loyal subjects, for with every problem, there is always a solution! Regardless of both sides factoring in and out of each other's opinions."

He looked with eccentric eyes to his fellow emperors, their faces showing that instant "don't do it" expressions. In this sense though, the Three Emperors had a short talk before the meeting, about mainly the outrageous idea he was not supposed to spout out in the meeting to come.

Not now. But, unfortunately for both of their respective viewpoints, they could only try to stop him from trying to explain his plan. "Emperor Baultus, please no! Not now."

Emperor Venus tried. "Baultus, please." Emperor Alvinor joined. "I have found a way to close the Rips! Yes, you heard me. A way to close the Rips, for good!" Everyone at the meeting table was dumbfounded by what Emperor Baultus just said.

"A way to close Rips? How? When?" These back thoughts rushed through Lord Gilmar's head like a hightailed speeder. "You see, during my long crusades in the Beyond, fighting through hordes of demons, saving countless worlds, I have found in my battles an answer to this crisis."

CHAPTER 9

Special cargo.

"There's nothing in this area, guardmaster!" Holyguard Nepo spent 2 minutes darting past and checking huge cargo containers at the same time with great speed, while also having to deal with annoying cultists attempting to halt him in his search.

Though no matter how much stood in his way, it will take more than dumb cultists, armed with plasma rifles and laser cannons, capable of melting most armor, to stop him. Left and right, every Demonik cultists were either trampled to a pulp or got repulsed by the sheer force of his charging manner, surrounded by the nigh-indestructible psychic shield. Another 40-foot container was coming up, labeled as food storage.

Despite this, he still had to check. They only had a limited amount of time to search for the special cargo, they had to make haste! He shouldered the massive weapon, made a fist, and tore through the metal like paper mache, only to find preserved micro-cheese bites and dura-toasts bags coming pouring out onto the floor, peering his head entirely. "Not this one." Nepo whispered to himself.

"Die, Holyguard scum!" Screamed a towering cultist from his rear, heavily armored, bringing down a vicious-looking broadsword, made from some bone matter, metal, and flesh strapped togetherly, covered and dripping with that black acidic substance.

Thanks to his psychic senses, Nepo dodged the oncoming attack just in time, the broadsword barely nicking his psychic energy shield.

He felt that something was different about this cultist, better yet the weapon should have shattered the minute it made contact with his psychic shield.

He best keeps his distance far from this follower of the Demonik, plays it safe, and opens fire on it with the Cleanser. "I don't have time for you, waste! Die, now!" Two projectiles beamed toward the target, quickly unholstered his sidearm and fired three proton rounds.

He never missed. But like a blurred image on a holoscreen, it vanished instantaneously from his sight, nowhere to be seen. *Teleportation? Lightspeed? Where is it?* Nepo's scanner could not detect anything, so he relied on his psychic senses to find out.

Swerving his head to the left, sensing an unseen threat charging toward him, sidestepped and concentrated on the fact that it was without a doubt the Demonik broadsword, once again. Only this time, invisible? No, just the broadsword. . .the entire cultist was invisible!

No wonder the scanners couldn't pick up any cloaking device of some kind, nor the built-in heat vision systems in his battle helm visor. Similar to the naturally Gifted users who could do the same, only this was nothing as he has ever felt.

This was different. It was like the Demonik cultist was almost gone from reality itself. He could see the floor beneath him become dented by the heavy slash of the broadsword, turning his Cleanser to the area where the cultist was and firing four shots.

Projectile after projectile, each hitting the target with deadly accuracy, hearing seared body parts flying onto different containers and some splatting on the floor.

And although he couldn't see the half-gooped corpse, he knew it was dead. BOOM! An explosion enveloped him from behind, the psychic shield taking the damage. But the blast was so strong it caused him to stagger in his stance, forcing Nepo to shoot out one of his arms for balance. Grunting in annoyance, eyes filled with anger and scanned the area behind.

"Damn, my senses must be off today." Commenting to himself. Nothing. . .yet. He heard the sound of loading grenade rounds and electoral switches to full auto, multiple footfalls not here on his level, but on the catwalk above him. But he couldn't see them!

Not even his heat vision scanner could pick them up.

As a natural holyguard reaction, in his literal nerves, he rolled fast to the nearest supportable cover that can withstand multiple grenade rounds and kept taking the punishment.

After all, these were no mere cheap containers made in the Hormik Territories, these were Baultus Empire-made. Reinforced to armor-worthy levels, built to take severe damage from ion cannons and handle the most horrible conditions known to humans.

In short, perfect cover for a powered armor holy warrior of Allsupra's faith, for a while at least.

One, two, or three rounds exploded on the container, shifting only a couple of inches from the explosive onslaught the invisible enemies were giving. Were they invisible to reality itself? Or were they cloaked by Demonik amplifications of some sort?

It reminded Nepo of an older mission that he and Craig were on a couple of months back, both a rescue mission and escorting an important figure in the Venus Empire. An elder commander by the name of Corus Balkor was 97 years old, who for some reason often visited Kildor Prime regularly and rambled on and on about his many, many wives across the Three Galaxies. Honestly, he didn't pay attention to those parts.

Wasn't briefed at all on why they had to escort him, except what he, Corus, told the young holyguards on why he was so important. Or more importantly, what he knew was vital to the Knowledge Priests of Scicana Prime. He could recall the memory in an instant, without any holdbacks.

"If you two're wondering why I'm so important to your fancy know-it-all priests back on Scenica, it's because I have info on possible new types of powers that are Gifted to those damn cultists the Demonik constantly use. A sorta veil on themselves to hide from reality or something like that. I should know. I killed one. Okay, I killed maybe five or more, but I barely remember because their bodies were all mush by the time I was done with them."

His origin supposedly traced back to the ancient days of Earth, like the Emperors and Empresses. With a slight unorthodox speech impediment he had, not to mention his unusual facial features, and very rectangularity to himself as a person, the old man was. . .interesting. Interesting, but his words were as true as a proud lion roaring.

"How I did it, ohhhhh. . .it wasn't easy, that's for sure! I can tell you this though, only a Gifted user, who had time to hone their vision to see certain dimensions at whim, can without doubt see them. Now to kill them is a little easy, cause they're still there and not there. Ya just have to believe hard enough and something physical should be there kinda! At least that's how I do it!" Corus Balkor, chuckled and patted the young holyguard on their uncovered heads, whipped a long cigar, and lit it, taking the soothing smoke with pleasure.

"Certain dimensions." In a glance, Hoyguard Nepo with his regular vision saw nothing but heard the warrior cultists running around, accruing like angered rats, cursing in the unholy tongue while unloading their hellish barrage on the container that served as a temporary cover.

"Certain dimensions. What did he mean?" Racking through definitions he knew, meanings he learned, texts he read, the history he'd seen, racking his brain cells in the concords of the many libraries the Sacred Order of Knowledge has built on numerous peaceful worlds has made.

Could he mean the different planes or dimensions that exist? 1st, 2nd, 3rd and 4th dimensions? If that was the case, then that meant he had to concentrate his sight significantly to the point where his eyes could potentially bleed if not temporary blindness or worse.

He knew and saw a 45-year-old Gifted user attempt this, however, he did not survive shortly after just peering into a fraction of the 4th dimension. He may not have survived but a holyguard such as himself?

Might have a surviving chance, with the combined power armor's healing systems and his already cemented Gifted abilities, Nepo might just have a chance. But if he didn't do this, what choice did he have?

By the sound of the impactful force of those grenade rounds, not to mention how it affected significant damage to his psychic shield with relative ease, cracking it, he knew that the rounds were either vexed, upgraded, or transformed to have volatile potency to destroy his shields and his armor in a matter of seconds. He can't let that happen.

He can't get hit by more than 2 rounds or else he will surely perish. He must succeed, he must survive. He had to find the special cargo at all costs! Tightening his free fist, he looked and gave a small prayer. Nepo, being a fully devoted believer of Alsupra, prayed true and hard despite having to be quick with it. "Alsupra, give me strength."

Holyguard Nepo, knowing that attempting this endeavor was gonna be extremely detrimental to his mind. So he prepared himself, went into a readied position, girded his loins, and hardened his already fluid psychic mind. The container shifted more and more, he could almost feel it close to shattering.

"Tan," Nepo said slowly to the power armor's guardian program. "In a few moments from now, I'll most likely be suffering from extreme cerebral damage and possibly start barking some insane nonsense about what I'll be seeing. But you, to the best of your power, won't allow that to happen. I have faith in you, Tan. You never failed me before, I know you won't fail me now."

Tan took time to form a response to his comrade in battle. Tan has been Nepo's faithful guardian program since his first assignment, healing every broken bone, muscle, and nerve that evil could throw at them. But to heal the mind continuously?

Scared Tan slightly. Since his sentient soul was pulled from the infinite realm of Jumpspace, he felt worried and scared at the same time, processing these feelings and thoughts faster than light itself. Tan had to suppress these feelings though and be logical and absolute with calculations that will save Nepo's life.

For a human to attempt to glimpse at the 4th dimension. . .is a deathwish for regular mortals. And it was not like Tan was experienced like a Paladin program, who could process their sight of multiple dimensions and transfer them to an actual viewable and survivable look into these realms.

"As you command, Holyguard Nepo. I will do my best." Tan replied. "I know." Nepo smiled, tilting his head to the catwalk above him. "I know."

Meanwhile, about 15 sections across from where Nepo is, was a structure that was constructed from containers stacked and moved by the Demonik cultists simulating some kind of fortress.

Like one, the stacked containers served as walls, where a few Demonik cultists were sentried and stood watch for anything or anyone who didn't worship the almighty powers of the Demonik Realm.

In this case, Amata and Craig. Before discovering this area though, they made clear already a couple of rows of containers, filled with numerous foods and supplies that have been well preserved over the long time it has been. These containers were also supposed to reach Markon 5, a small cluster of moons near Baultus Prime. At all costs. At least, that's what the manifesto reads on them.

After stampeding and slaying over 30 Demonik cultists in her path, not to mention the certain types of supplies that are in these containers, Holyguard Craig couldn't help but feel . . . confused. She usually never feels this way at all when facing hordes of enemies of the Three Empires, but then again, when does anything make sense when fighting the Demonik.

Their strategies in battle have been known to be unpredictable at all times but over the years, a basic pattern has recurred. Take over a singular planet with a small populace, obviously susceptible to Demonik corruption, and like an unnoticed spark, spreads from planet to planet in a matter of days like wildfire. And it would make sense why they would need to salvage whatever ships they can find to support their efforts in the war, even though they made their own.

But why this B.E.T.S of all of them? Whatever this special cargo must be was worth the piles of cultist warriors that she and Amata killed getting here. She almost forgot something too. Switching her view from the makeshift fortress to a mangled corpse of a high-ranking Demonik cultist, his lower half completely smashed to a mulchy pulp from Amata, and plasma rifle parts were scattered across the floor.

Then her vision locked on to the corpse of one the dead engineers that worked on this carrier. Still keeping her eyes on the sentries that moved constantly, Craig never lost cover once when she went back for the two bodies, Amata did not worry her mind when she glanced back to see what Craig was going back for.

First, Craig knelt to the dead engineer, his upper chest riddled with holes, cleanly seared by laser bolts while the rest of his limbs were burnt to a crisp as was his head. Too bad his fire-resistant suit didn't cover much of his face, but still, upon examining closer, she noticed he died immediately after the laser bolts hit his chest area. Placing a hand on his chest, feeling for the holotag that he would've carried on him at all times. After finding it, she read it quietly to herself.

"Greg. Greg Allem."Craig sighed deeply."Husband and father of two children, hailing from the Inner Systems in the Venus Empire. Age:34. Race: Half Breed."

Holotags kept track of personal information of the person, whether it was the date on when they fired a gun to what brave actions they did in battle.

She continued to read, and more and more holographic information on the engineer popped into her visor. Each file is scanned, confirmed, and copied to her downloads. Aiming her left arm at the neck area of the burnt corpse, a huge sharp metal syringe came jolting out with speed and jammed it into his spine.

For research purposes known only to her and one other person, which was a mystery to even Guardmaster Ricardo, Craig conducted multiple experiments. And yes, despite how uncanny and questionable she gets when it comes to fulfilling her research, Guardmaster Ricardo never questions her on her methods.

Ripping leftover lungs and draining spinal fluid from corpses once in a while was a part of that research. Craig occasionally, depending on the amount of damage done to the body, would take blood samples, bone tissue, and mostly brain matter, from dead Demonik cultists. Then again, occasionally. "Why are you taking his spinal fluid? He's a charred corpse, Craig. Nothing more to know about how he died." Amata asked her. Craig nodded and said.

"Yes, Amata. I know how he died. But I need to know why the limbs were only burnt and not his torso. I just need to know. Because you and I both know that the Demonik is unpredictable in everything they do from how they attack in battle to their ranking system, even their supposed gods they believe."

Over many of her battles, the piles of bodies she saw, the wounds they died from, and ringing memories of pain rushed into her mind. Looking back on these old memories, she remembered a lecture by an old knowledge priest on Scienca Prime.

"Years of knowledge I have accumulated in my lifetime, seeing both mind-bending horrors to astronomical miracles on the battlefield and after. But today is different, my young students. Subject: The Demonik

Realm and its followers. To understand the Demonik, is to understand chaos and madness itself. Which could be nigh impossible for even the strongest minds to understand. As I said yesterday, the cultists who follow the Demonik can fight with supernatural strength, even on an empty stomach. They need not feed off the sustenance of this universe, some would say. Rather they feed off the negative energies of others. Pain is one of their primary ones. This means they don't have to eat any food at all At least from my perspective and research!"

Blinking twice, Craig looked back to a blue-lined container, filled to the brim with duratoasts."I mean, why?" Craig whispered. "They don't even need to eat regular food, those cultist bastards. So why? Just for this special cargo of sorts? Something's at work here, Amata." Amata looked to Craig, with a face of disconcert, underneath her battlehelm. "Something's always at work, Craig." An ear-piercing shriek came from one of the cultists, who locked his targeting reticle on Amata, who had her head popped out of cover when she was talking with Craig.

Pulling the trigger, his rotted finger squeezing slowly, his plasma rifle shot. With great speed the plasma bolt came closer and closer to Amata's head, bouncing uselessly off her psychic shields. "Blast! That was dumb!" Amata dropped to the floor in an instant and retook cover and shouted to her fellow holyguard. "One spotted me!" In anger with this reaction, the sentry got up from his sniper position and yelled to the other cultists in the fortress.

"Over here! Over here! Holyguard on the northern side! Kill them!" Within a single minute, poured-out Demonik cultist warriors, armed with plasma rifles, rained hell in the direction of containers where Amata and Craig took cover behind, some already trying to flank their position.

Having this suppressing plasma fire these Demonik cultists were giving Craig and Amata, combined with the autocannon mounted on one of the catwalks guardrails overhead, it was best they stayed behind cover for the time being until they came up with a plan. "They got some heavy firepower, Craig!" Amata shouted, a stray plasma bolt whizzed past her shoulder, bouncing off her psychic shield and dissipating into tiny energy particles.

"Those plasma rifles." Craig noticed. "Their Omnobuild, gen-12 models. Used primarily by militia forces in the Baultus Empire for their overcharged capabilities, remember? Despite the massive damage they do on energy shields, they still require huge magazines and power packs. Meaning. . ." Amata chimed in both agreement and remembrance. "That the weapons themselves can be disabled by a long-range disarranger for a short amount of time!" Craig nodded.

"Giving us only that autocannon to deal with, Amata." Omnobuild Corporation. Responsible for manufacturing and producing, designing hundreds if not thousands of weapons, vehicles, city, and planetary shield designs in the Baultus Empire, originating from a small unnamed star cluster. Even though a lot of their weapons are considered outdated by a few races in the Three Empires. Still, if the technology they created still did its intended purpose, then it did its purpose. And many of the Demonik cultist warriors use any type of weapons they could find at first, over time creating their own or even having crafted weapons given to them by the Demonik Gods themselves.

"Alright, I'm activating my disarranger signal in their area." Amata pressed a medley of buttons on her wrist gauntlet, switching two switches that activated a large blue button in the center. Without a second thought, Amata pressed it and within seconds the plasma rifles they were firing abruptly jammed violently, electrocuting their bodies entirely, some even falling, screaming in agony.

Both holyguard smiled in reaction, but behind them came the flanking cultists, armed with laser cannons and readying themselves to attack Amata and Craig. However, just as they opened fire, Craig sensed their filthy presence long before they came to their position, unclipped her impact hammer, and threw it at the ground where the cultists were. This attack created a powerful shockwave that not only destroyed the floor but also sent the Demonik cultist flying 20 feet in the air in all directions. With her free hand, she summoned her impact hammer back to her and catching it, it came back to her with great speed.

"Gravity slam!" She comically shouted. "Now then, Amata . . .let us bring death to these foolish followers!" In a fluid motion, Craig and Amata both turned in the direction of the mini fortress and charged with devastating fury, determined to find out what they were guarding behind those container walls.

The roaring sound of constant plasma turret ripples and Konami cannons from the outside could be heard from where they were running, meaning that Captain Zendaya must be dealing with the other Demonik reinforcements that their guardmaster mentioned earlier.

Amata counted the plasma blasts, separating each one from the other in her mind with her increased hearing. "One, two, three. . .by the Emperors." Amata said. "Captain Zendaya is holding off more than 15 Demonik battleships! She won't last long if we don't hurry to find that special cargo soon! Come on!" As they gained speed in their charge toward the fortress, dodging the auto cannon's plasma bolts that ricocheted off the floor, Craig looked to her fellow holyguard, with a confused expression.

"Why? Do you doubt Captain Zendaya's skill in naval warfare?" Amata looked at Craig sternly. "I do not doubt her skill in naval warfare! I doubt her-" Two plasma bolts made contact with her psychic shield, cracking it severely. Meaning that Amata was losing focus on generating and forming the psychic shield that protected her. Although this didn't stop her at all in her path, Craig did call out to her when seeing this happen and shouted.

"Amata!" Amata grunted with frustration. "I'm fine, Craig. Let's just keep going and focus on our objectives in that fortress!" Praying to

Alsupra, Amata whispered in the Moderian tongue. "Please, Alsupra. Ancestors, let this be where it is." It needed to be the special cargo. It just had to be, because they were running out of time fast, both of them could feel it.

She knew that Guardmaster Ricardo had faith in Captain Zendaya, some might say too much faith whether it being her head first into the battle strategy to consistent insubordination to certain levels of higher authority, excluding Guardmaster Ricardo and a few unmentioned others in her notebook of self-thought.

Looking up the history surrounding Captain Zendaya since Guardmaster Ricardo first met her or more likely found her in a dirty alleyway, on some corrupted independent planet, drunk and depressed beyond compare. But with great pity and mercy for Zendaya, he rehabilitated her and took care of her, eventually reinstating her position as navy captain in the Baultus Empire. Even though Captain Zenday was much older than Guardmaster Ricardo's team of young holyguards, it still left Amata with many doubts about Captain Zendaya as a capable person to handle what holyguard see or do in the battle against the Demonik's many unholy forces.

Sensing what issues were wrong with Zendaya, many of them related to her mental or even worse emotional health to say the least. Whenever she was around the other young holyguard, they could feel that something was off about her presence but paid no mind to it at all. They simply shrugged it off as she was probably having a bad day with another, in her words, a lousy superior on the navy comm channel or she just had bottled up emotions about her past that she didn't feel like she needed to share with anyone.

But Amata, being the devoted religious warrior she is, needed to know more about Zendaya, just as a precaution. Unfortunately, whenever she respectfully pressured the matter on high-ranking officers and knowledge priests, they simply told her not to look into Zendaya's past anymore. Even other guardmasters told her the same thing, excluding, of course, Guardmaster Ricardo, who told Amata this.

"I see you have taken interest in finding out more about Captain Zendaya's past of late. I sadly, however, can only tell this. It was an incident so terrible, it happened long before you were born and it was covered up by the Sacred Order of Knowledge with good intentions. But know this Amata, the only reason I keep her around is that I know her family's history and to keep a close watch on her, as a precaution. I have faith that you will keep this to yourself, Amata."

Amata has kept silent since then but continues in her search to find out more about Zendaya. She scoffed at herself, remembering the mission at hand. "Focus, focus! Find the special cargo! We're running out of time." A few Demonik cultists stood in her way to stop Amata, only for them to be backhanded by her superhuman strength, flinging them to containers like ragdolls. Craig just shoulder-charged three of the Demonik cultists into the air. They reached the southern side of the fortress and tore through the containers easily, stomping on farming tools, pottery, and seeds, exiting out into the inner part of the fortress and found themselves in the presence of the Demonik cultists who were terrified that they reached them. Some could barely make out words, trembled, dropping their disabled weapons, and ran to the entrance to flee from the two holyguard that towered above them like giants.

Craig threw her impact hammer at the entrance area where the fleeing Demonik cultists were, atomizing their physical forms to nothing. Ten seconds of silence grew, leaving only four Demonik cultists who remained, unfazed by their powerful entry and growled viciously, glaring at both Amata and Craig through those visorless helmets they wore. Red drool dripped and they kept their mouths wide, licking their tongue across their face in hungry-esque mannerisms and speaking.

"If you think that the special cargo of Emperor Baultus is here, you're wrong." It was a female, but one could barely tell the difference with their guttural voices. The female cultist laughed in amusement, dropping the plasma rifle to the floor, and unsheathing two jagged metal swords that were not made from this universe. Twirling her swords and slashing them in the air, she held up one of them, pointing it at Craig.

"You came here for nothing, you foolish holyguard. None of you will get off this ship alive. The special cargo is Demonik by right, so she belongs to our gods and our gods alone will decide what to do with her. As for you. . . " A smug smile formed on the female cultist's face, the other cultists around them slowly joined, moving in with inhuman melee weapons as they crept closer and closer to Amata and Craig. "Prepare for your deaths, holyguard!"

In an unnatural leap of movement, the female cultist sprang fast at Amata, her swords coming down with tremendous speed, in a chopping motion. Then in a sudden jerk, she stopped in mid-air, dropping her swords and reaching for her neck. Being choked by an unseeable force, she could feel that nothing was holding her in place but at the same time, there was something slowly squeezing her throat. Seeing a yellow aura around the one who was choking her (Amata), it must have been the Gifted ability of telekinesis.

Spitting in anger, struggling to ungrip herself from this slow death, feeling her oxygen get cut off bit by bit, she cursed at Amata. "Damn you holyguard and your accursed Gifts! May the demons of the Demonik Gods feast on your souls-" Crunch! Her throat was gone with a closed fist from Amata and with a swipe of her hand, she used her Gifted ability of telekinesis to throw out of the fortress-like a piece of crumpled paper.

A cultist roared, angered, and at the same time, all three Demonik cultists charged with their melee weapons high. Back to back, Amata wielded her axes in a guard position, Craig swiped her impact hammer with her right hand, and on her left forearm, a plasma arm cannon, primed and charged. "Let's get this over with and check this fortress quickly after, okay Craig?" Amata said, then with a slight smile, Craig replied. "Agreed." She sighed softly. "Pray to Alsupra that Benji and Guardmaster Ricardo has better luck than us."

CHAPTER 10

Krennic.

Not letting down his guard once, Holyguard Benji made sure the engineer was safe from harm at all costs, but at the same time he had to fight somehow. Kneeling on the floor, he knew how cruel the forces of the Demonik were, they would most definitely try to use her against him. But he was a Holyguard and such petty tactics would not work against someone like Benji. Good thing that Guardmaster Ricardo was with him, otherwise this would've been extra difficult to protect her. Guardmaster Ricardo used his manipulation over lightning, transferred it through the proton shotgun, and fired upon the demons who leaped towards Benji and clawed into his psychic shields.

Since Guardmaster Ricardo never missed a target, the demons he shot, combined with both proton and electrical energy surging through the shell caused them to blow up into charred bits, scattered across the floor, and prickled Benji's psychic shield. He wanted If this is what it felt like to be helpless in a fight, then Benji didn't like it at all. Not one bit. Even though he knew that Guardmaster Ricardo didn't mind at all, simply because he was just trying to protect the dramatized civilian.

The young woman had felt the power of a Demonik demon. He looked down at her, the unconscious engineer shifted slightly in his armored arms, and a quiet whimper escaped her small lips as she did so. "Forgive me, guardmaster. I feel like I am not supporting you enough in helping-" Guardmaster Ricardo interrupted him, placed a free hand on his shoulder, and said to him. "Don't think that."

"Benji, you have every right to be concerned for her safety. Take care of her and follow my lead at all times. Support me in any way you can try but at all times, keep her safe. That is my order, Benji. Alright?" Guardmaster Ricardo could see young Benji took time to think deeply about what he said, looking at the engineer with gentle eyes, he shut tightly.

Benji inhaled slowly, sighing, and said. "Yes, sir." Guardmaster Ricardo smiled, activated his Heavenly Father Blade, and unhooked the massive barrel of his automatic proton scattergun, the ejected cylindrical battery clinked on the floor behind him. Blue smoke and empty. It was a break-barrel model of the auto-proton scattergun, resembling some old design from Ancient Earth.

Not exactly a double barrel, but had lever action built into its handle area for quick firefights. In a flawless motion, he reloaded the weapon without effort and swerved his head to the seemingly endless rows of red, blue, and orange-colored stacked containers, trying to pinpoint the location of the special cargo. For a regular mortal, this would be similar to trying to find a minute piece of fine jewelry amongst other jewels.

The distance between the beginning and end area of the cargo bay area was more than 1000 miles long. "Just check the manifest data computer, some would say." He whispered with a comedic tone. "If only it were that easy." Unfortunately, as it may sound, it wasn't easy at all. Most B.E.T.S.(Baultus Empire Trading Ships) containers are most often, usually manually loaded by humanoid and android personnel.

Wearing mech suits that can carry these containers into rows or giant mechanical claws that organize them according to color, with certain ones equipped with gravity controllers to make them weightless. Still, all the manifesto knowledge was kept safely in the mind of the captain. Who, at the moment, could not be found or was most likely dead.

Guardmaster Ricardo, the armored collar circumferencing around his neck, felt as if someone's breath came down his nape, diseased and unnerving. He didn't show fear though from this, but his curiosity did peak. With a raised eyebrow, turned around to find nothing but the continuous darkened stacks and rows of containers. Sensing some unseen presence near their location, vulturous eyes watching them from a shadowy distance.

He suspected it was a cultist sniper at first, but as he concentrated harder, whoever or whatever was watching felt evil but it didn't feel like an evil he ever encountered before in his life. It didn't reek of the Demonik nor did it have any good intentions toward him, Benji, and the engineer. Even though he couldn't see it, Guardmaster Ricardo knew it was there. It just watched them, from the shadows. Prominent but subtle. He stood there for more than 40 seconds searching the darkness, before turning to Benji, kneeling to his level and saying. "Let us press on, Benji. Let us press on." Giving his hand to help Benji up, clasping hands tightened as he assisted the young holyguard to his footing.

Out of nowhere, above them, screaming bloody murder a raging cultist towards the two holyguard. Armored in ravaged Baultus Empire trooper gear, the crysamite was cracked, revealing the torn brown skin suit. The black, blood-garnished impact hammer came down with such horrendous force, destroying the floor, revealing wiring and all. But Benji and Guardmaster Ricardo sensed the cultist just at the last second and jumped backward, metal fragments shooting across the armor, pricking and flattening against their psychic shields.

How did they sense this cultist earlier? The Demonik cultist got so close to them that it even left Guardmaster Ricardo surprised. "By the Emperors!" Grunting, Benji landed back on his feet and regained his ground, checking the engineer if she suffered damage. Finding nothing, he sighed and held her tight in one arm in a hugging position making sure she was safe and secure. After doing this, he summoned the Sword of Moned to his hand with one of his Gifted abilities, telekinesis. Struggling at first, Benji focused harder for it seemed that the weapon didn't want to come to his hand at first.

Benji grunted. "You resist me?" With determined eyes, a loud hum grew louder, and then wham! The sword came into his grip. With a smile, he held the Sword of Moned and pointed it at the drooling cultist. "Do not think you stand a chance against us, slave of the Demonik! You see this?" The Demonik cultist switched his view, observing the sword that Benji wielded in his right hand, glowing with an aura of pure light, it made the cultist blink with interest.

Moving its head in a slow catlike manner, tilting its head and then switching back to face him. With a gurgle, the cultist spoke. "What of it, holyguard scum?" Guardmaster Ricardo had both his weapons drawn, his auto-proton scattergun pointed at the Demonik follower and his Heavenly Father Blade in a tall guard position. From Ricardo's view, an unseen power about this Demonik cultist stood before them, possibly enough to deal significant damage to both holyguard if they tried to move now. So to be safe, with a small nod signaling Benji, to wait on his command.

"This sword. . ." Benji continued. "My father, Jesse Foemasta, wielded this. The Sword of Moned!" A fearful gasp left its pungent mouth, looking once again at the sword with dilated eyes. "The Sword of Moned!" The Demonik cultist trembled. Backing up to a nearby container, glared at Ricardo and screamed. "So you're the one my lord has been seething over for many days now! The lost relic, hidden by the Demonik's gaze for some time now! Killer of Legions and Beholders Bane is known by us. You boy!"

It pointed at Benji, with glowing eyes now. "What you have in your possession, you carry my lord's-" Burst! Its head exploded, black bits of brain matter and skull splattered all over their psychic shields, Benji jerked in surprise but Guardmaster Ricardo, unfazed by this, sensed an ominous, dark figure behind them. "By the Emperors." Benji said. Both he and Guardmaster Ricadro in a quick reaction took a defensive stance and faced this mysterious person.

It was a woman, human, and looked like she barely left out of her twenties. Her hair was dyed blue and her eye color was blue also. She walked closer and closer to them, stumbling and struggling to stay on her feet. Examining closer, the two holyguard noticed this woman was wearing a bionic cryosuit, a similar design from the Alvinor Empire.

Half dazed but still seeming enthralled by the mere sight of them, the woman attempted to speak but collapsed before she could utter a single word. Sensing signs mostly signs of physical exhaustion on the woman, Guardmaster Ricardo sprinted, holstered his weapons, and caught her just in time. She groaned, placing a hand on her forehead, and sighed in relief.

"Who is she, guardmaster?" Benji asked. Her pale body was cold to the touch, tired eyes met the guardmaster, and bright blue met dark brown. But the minute he touched her, he could feel a powerful surge of Demonik energy coursing through his entire body, having a volatile reaction with his Gifted energy.

Undoubtedly powerful, but unharmful to his body, mind, and soul. This immediately shocked the grandmaster's mind, having seen many things over the years but this, this was different. It wasn't a demon, nor was she possessed by one or more.

This energy, despite it being Demonik, came from her alone. As if she could manipulate or transfer Demonik energy through her very being, but it seemed as if she did not know her powers. . .yet. Benji felt and could see the guardmaster's very soul not contorted, but bent by the sudden rush of Demonik energy that shot through him, sudden and inconceivable to even Benji's mind. At first, he thought that Guardmaster Ricardo was under a spiritual attack upon his soul, reaching for his sheathed sword; he was halted in his actions when the guardmaster gave him a fierce command so loud, that shook the very atmosphere. "Cease, Benji!"

Extreme psychic energy poured out of his eye sockets, channeling lightning uncontrollably to his surroundings, rippling and bouncing across the ground's surface. Roaring with the upheaval of the foreign emotions, thoughts, memories, and the woman's voice within his head, trying to speak to him in some form of language from. . .Ancient Earth.

Containers nearby were slowly crushed and pushed by the forceful intake of unknown knowledge his mind succumbed to. She was trying to communicate to him through the mind, a form of telepathy similar to what he and some Gifted users would use if they wanted certain conversations to be unlistened and unnoticed. Private talks some say. He tried picking out multiple phrases, and strange compound words that he hasn't heard of before except library studies on Sciencia Prime. Some of the things she was inputting into his mind had similar words from the old texts that dated back before even the Three Emperors.

"Must. . .elaspe. . . the gates." The very words stretched his mind, brain cell to brain cell, by just trying to translate to an understandable tongue that the guardmaster could understand. There was more. "I. . .am. . .the. . . .cargo. Baultus. . .knows me. . .as Krennic. Remember Krennic." She fainted, all the energy that both of them were producing ceased in an instant, leaving Guardmaster Ricardo open-eyed and panting. He looked at her once again, examining her face closely.

"Krennic." He whispered. "Why do I know that name from someplace?" Benji walked towards him and said. "Guardmaster. I sense you suffered no physical damage to your body. But your soul. . ." Benji paused. "Your soul shines differently now, sir." Guardmaster Ricardo had a face of deep thought. He had to confirm what she told him. He just had to be sure. If this woman is truly who she supposedly says she is, even though he couldn't sense any form of Demonik deceiving, he just had to be sure.

Because if she truly is the "special cargo" that Emperor Baultus needed, then he can give the order to the rest of his team to cease their search and be recalled via jump teleportation back to the Omori.

From there they can fall back to Moses-1, recuperate, and send a coded message to Emperor Baultus about obtaining the special cargo. He looked at her naked feet, covered in a slimy gel substance, and could see a long trail of it that led it to her possible point of origin. "Benji." He said. "Follow me."

All the faces across the meeting table were left confused or blank because they had no idea who this person was. This woman known as Emma Krennic was known up to this very point during the meeting, with information on her and all. "Forgive me my emperor, but who is this Emma Krennic? Is she a descendant of one the Royal Human Houses or a distant, distant cousin to you perhaps?" The Lycan warchief said concernedly, with Emperor Baultus replying to her. "Neither, milady. Neither at all. You see, it has been confirmed by me and my fellow emperors that Emma Krennic dates back to Earth. Ancient Earth."

Emperor Alvinor moved his gravity throne forward to align his position with the other emperors and said. "Meaning that she originated from Earth, like us. Born and raised." Princess Xingla's tentacles fluttered after he said this. "As old as you, my emperors?" Emperor Alvinor made a face. "Well, no. In fact, after taking DNA samples and running numerous biology tests, she is indeed older than.. .well. . .us. By 100 centuries to be precise." Royal cousin family members and the military leaders gasped at this. This left all of them murmuring amongst each other, especially Princess Xingla and Lord Gilmar.

In all their life, they have never heard of any living being older than the Three Emperors themselves, the exceptions being when they read in history books that there is evidence of many obscure races older than mankind, one of them being the revered Celestials. Living for thousands upon thousands of years and have ignored even the most drastic conflicts that happened in the universe because they deemed it "it was unnecessary for us to help at the time." Then again, there are very, very few races that behave like this. Very few. But even so, a human older than the Three Emperors themselves?

It was almost as inconceivable as the creation of the infinite universe. Wanting to ask so many questions, not being able to withhold them, Lord Gilmar came first. “Emperor Alvinor. You don’t mean she’s older than the rest of you, right? A hundred centuries? If she really is this old, how is she still alive?” Lord Gilmar prolonged the word to show his attempt to understand more about this Krennic. “Better yet, who is this Emma Krennic?!”

Lord Gilmar scanned the entire table, pointing at his relatives from the other Royal Cousin Houses related to Emperor Baultus. “Cause it seems like no one here, especially any of the Royal Houses, have any knowledge of the name whatsoever.” He looked to the Bolter princes and princesses and mockingly scoffed at one of them. “Not surprising really.”

Showing spite in their faces, a Bolter princess shot back at Lord Gilmar immediately. “Did you just title the Bolter Family a bunch of idiots?!” Leaning back into his chair, he replied. “No, no of course not. Just the men, I mean.” Anger dangled upon the Bolters who attended the meeting, one of the princes growled with frustration at the Victorian-born human. Princess Xingla could smell the air change drastically, things were getting tense fast between the Victorian lord and the Bolters. But all this tension ceased when Emperor Venus slammed his mighty, shouting so loud that the room shook violently.

“Enough all of you! By God, if I hadn’t promised your great, great, great grandparents that I’d watch over you all, I would without a second thought erase the literal concepts of contempt, anger, and hatred for each other, replace them with some uncanny fantastical feelings for one another. Now please, no more arguing, and just listen to what we are trying to explain to everyone present.”

Silence filled the room. Baultus moved his gravity throne near Venus, his face with a comical yet sarcastic look on it, and used his telepathy. "Vash, that's no way to talk to my cousin's descendants. They're young and stupid but are still family, c'mon you know this." Venus sighed. "I know, I know. Sorry, my friend." Baultus nodded in response, switching his view slowly back to Alvinor, and nodded to him to continue.

"As I was saying, Emma Krennic is indeed older than us. None of you know her or have any knowledge of the name because you weren't there to witness the strange disappearance firsthand. Not even us, for it happened in the 21st century, on Earth before any of us were even born, a mere children's horror story to some, to others a darker, darker mystery. The very name Krennic was unnerving, their entire family legacy, the supposed unspeakable acts they committed against all life. Even after all the things the Krennics have done, covering their tracks throughout Earth's history, only one truly good soul attempted to come out and expose them for who they were. That soul, that person, that human, was Emma Krennic."

Some raised eyebrows, others had pouty lips, hands in pondering positions. "Unfortunately, she didn't. Before she revealed the truth about her own family, she disappeared." Princess Xingla clacked and clicked her mandible-like appendages and said in a soft voice, rubbing her hands together slowly, feeling unnerved.

"Disappeared, my emperor?" Emperor Alvinor nodded to her. "Yes, Princess Xingla. Disappeared, without a trace. During the Common Era days of Ancient Earth, she was considered a missing person in historical documents, how she disappeared was another unexplained phenomenon in its own right. Most people believed she was dead, with no evidence to link back to the Krennic Family. But after all this time, of all the places, on one of the many crusades that Emperor Baultus has done, he found her. Lost, confused, and left terrified on a tiny planet in a volatile chaotic star cluster, beyond the reign of the Three Empires, where hordes upon hordes of pure form demons guarded her unforgivingly."

Emperor Baultus interrupted. "Even more interesting is when I found her, she was standing in front of a Demonik Rip, with demons on the other side. And when I sensed them, they were petrified with fear and anger in the mere presence of not me, but Emma herself. Even I could feel the unlimited energy flow throughout her body, uncontrollably but harmless to me. More surprisingly, it was Demonik energy she was channeling through her, and an incantation from her the Rip was closed!" Emperor Baultus clasped his hands together loudly. "She used the Demonik tongue to close it though. Which means. . ."

Ten feet away from the meeting table, the large metal doors swung ajar, catching everyone except the Three Emperors and their Honorguards off guard. It was not opened by hand but by other Gifted means, someone so gifted that it made the entire room quiver, slightly similar to the Three Emperors powers, but nothing compared to their godlike presence.

His presence felt like what some would call a devout incarnate, forged from the blue fires of abuse, reborn out of the ashes of Ancient Earth, and ordained by all who follow him as their one, true teacher of the holy word of Alsupra divine truth. He came today after hearing the word of this meeting from Alsupra himself.

Unannounced and uninvited. As their duty as the Honorguard, they were ordered by the Three Emperors themselves not to halt or interfere in his path at all times. This man, clad in his gloriously golden power armor, a giant to regular humans, is Joshua Xanths, Supreme Leader of the Holyguard. He finished Baultus's sentence. "Only someone who can speak the heathenous tongue and survive can close the Rips the Demonik use as trans-dimensional gateways for their untold legions."

Joshua looked at where they sat in the gravity thrones, the Three Emperors, their faces stern, eyebrows furrowed with disapproval from his untold arrival. His afro fluctuated with spiritual energy, smiled, bowing low to the floor itself, and said. "My emperors, it is an honor to be in your godlike presence once again." Emperor Venus can see his old friend, bowing to him and saying to him. "Joshua."

CHAPTER 11

Newfound knowledge.

"You're sure of this, Benji?" Amata asked through her helmet's built-in long-range com channel, enabling them to talk without actually having to be near each other. Picking up faster-than-light voice channels that can reach up to an entire planetary system. Good thing too, for Amata and Craig, were quite busy at the moment and had difficulty understanding what Benji was telling them over their helms, especially with the swarming Demonik cultist chanting that unholy tongue before striking. Amata had a grip on a demon, being choked by her unforgiving grip and snap! She threw the body in Craig's direction and could see the demon's limp body blackened and burned in an instant with the mind-lightning that

Craig directed toward it. Ducking a plasma grenade that exploded in front of her, tickling her psychic shield, barely moving from her battle stance. Craig swung her impact hammer fast and hard at the oncoming cultists who shot their plasma rifles at her, yelling they're all before they became pulpy black mist. Amata dodged a missile fired from a Nozerian militia missile launcher, primitive tech but deadly. The Demonik cultist pulled back the second handle, the mechanisms activated and loaded the next missile into the barrel, and fired away again.

"Hold on, Benji!" Amata grunted, backflipped, and went behind the nearest container. More explosions went off from the missiles impacting the container, the cultist laughing and taunting her. She grunted in annoyance and saw Craig getting swarmed by five demons, slashing their claws at her psychic shield, almost cracking it. Charged with spiritual energy, Craig created a shockwave that blasted all of them away. Amata could hear on Benji's end that he was running. He continued.

"My eyes do not deceive me, Amata. The special cargo, the one that Emperor Baultus ordered us to retrieve, is a human named Emma Krennic. I searched through hundreds of files on the name, but nothing came up. Nothing at all." Benji grunted, indicating that he must've been battling on his end also. Multiple demons can be heard through his channel in the background, being slashed and torn apart by the Sword of Moned she sensed.

A demon screamed in burning agony, and the sound of blazing fire cascaded with it, eventually disappearing into silence. Gasping from surprise, he made a remarking sound, which he wouldn't do unless something caught him off guard. "By the Emperors!" He complimented the Sword of Moned, smiling with this humble discovery. "That never happened before!" Amata raised an eyebrow at this, the explosions getting worse behind her, and said.

"What? What happened, Benji?" Another demon tried to ambush him from behind, but it was a pointless move when the demon met the Sword of Moned. Face to face, literally. Once again, another demon was engulfed in blue flames. "The Sword of Moned burns the demon's flesh! Even as I wave it about now, the blade is covered in an amazing blue fire, I feel no heat being exchanged from it also. I wish you were here to see it, for it is a truly magnificent sight to behold, Amata. But enough about my father's weapon for the Celestial's sake!" Noticing seven pairs of beady white eyes in the darkness around him.

"Hold on a moment." Noticing a multitude of black tentacles slithering and violently slamming against his psychic shield. Benji held the engineer close to his chest, securing her and making sure that she was safe. One slimy tentacle slammed impacting after another, and his psychic shield cracked from the immense force of two demons made, their pitch-black faces contorted by the large grins they wore, having many tentacles protruded from their heads and used them to break through his psychic shield, wrapping them around his legs, attempting to envelop him.

Sneering and giggling at the young imposing holyguard, Benji could only feel annoyed by their unholy presence. A tentacle nearly touched her exposed feet, writhed in anger at them even trying to bring harm to the innocent woman, and moved before its slimy tentacles could touch her. One of them laughed and commented. “Oh goodness me, my brothers. Isn’t that the girl that got violated by that defiler a while ago?” One of the demons drooled in excitement.

“Yes, it is, yes it is! Oh, I remember every single bone and muscle in her body, stretching and expanding beyond human limits from that defiler demon.” It sighed with a lustrous tone. “Ohh. . .if only I was a Bregori demon, I could savor the moment again, again and again without end. A true loop. But alas, we are nothing more than children of Uncanik, born from the Demonik god Uncany. Like our tentacles, we know no limit to our coiling grasp and there is no secret or darkness or lie that is not known by us or her, Uncany. Do you know who you carry with you, mortal?”

The demon quivered with claws covering its putrid black lips, mockingly, Benji remained silent and kept his guard up, increasing the psychic shield, thickening it. The tentacles that did get through were immediately severed and incinerated to ashes. “She is a nobody now, but she is one of the last of an intoxicating bloodline that should’ve ended long ago on that annoying, green planet of yours.”

Benji scoffed in disbelief but noted it just in case. His compassionate eyes locked onto the engineer he safely held, seeing her and processing the demon's horrible words. In the eyes of a holyguard, innocence, true innocence, could be physically seen in their soul as comforting, warm, blinding sunlight light.

"You demons are nothing more than proud liars. All of you. Granted, the possible knowledge you unholy beings have accumulated over the years of conquering the untold number of universes, I could only imagine."

Girding his loins, he prepared himself, tensed his thighs, and focused his view on a couple of stacked containers above him, where Guardmaster Ricardo had charged spiritual energy in his left fist, waiting patiently for young Benji to move. Giving a hand signal that only a holyguard would know, Benji held the engineer closer and tighter for the upcoming action he was going to take.

"Years?" A demon snickered. "Years, mortal? How about eons, to be more exact. You can't possibly imagine how many universes we have corrupted, how many innocent lives we have taken and converted. For we take pleasure in the great pain of others!" The demons surrounding his psychic shield coiled back, rattling, just aching to dig their sharp, disgusting tentacles hurt the two humans. . .extremely.

"You two will die, like the mortals you are!" Launching themselves forward with inhuman speed, roaring and squealing, their black drool melting the floor beneath them. Doing a fast 360 spin, glancing at each demon, targeting them. With a single bound, jumping with such strength that the floor broke apart, momentarily stopping the demons in their tracks.

Using the Sword of Moned, sliced straggling tentacles managed to get a hold of one of his legs. Grunting in anger, he made extra sure that none of those demons would follow them. Directing all of the charged spiritual energy, Guardmaster Ricardo let out a thunderous roar so loud and imposing, that even the demons were shaken by his voice. Their beady eyes showed great fear, knowing their very physical existence in this universe was coming to a quick end. Right. . .now!

Like a raging river, pure blue energy rushed swiftly on both sides, capturing and drowning the demons, painfully erasing their physical bodies one body part at a time. The demon's scream quickly became gurgled in the Gifted energy that manipulated to be in this waterlike form, spliced with the enormous amount of spiritual energy he stored beforehand.

When someone is Gifted, they could access two main forms of universal energy that flowed and lived throughout the entire infinite universe: the Physical and Spiritual. Sometimes, when a Gifted user had access to both forms of energy, it granted them a wide display of powers, perfectly balanced. Guardmaster Ricardo used what many races would call manipulation of energy.

Benji landed on the container where Guardmaster Ricardo was, glancing back down over the edge, seeing the energy being dispersed across the floor below and slowly dissipating into nothingness. Seeing the engineer was safe and unharmed, Benji sighed, turned to his guardmaster, walked to his side, and said. "Guardmaster Ricardo, If the woman you are holding is indeed the special cargo Emperor Baultus sent us to find, then shouldn't I contact the others and inform Captain Zendaya to recall us back to the Omori?"

Guardmaster continued his gaze, concentrating on whatever caught his eye. Benji noticed this too. "Guardmaster?" Benji asked with concern. He could sense in the guardmaster something that troubled him deeply, a feeling of mild confusion. "I knew it. . ." Guardmaster Ricardo said slowly. Benji's brow furrowed, then in a moment. . .the sight that lay before them.

"A cryo pod." Benji remarked. "That explains the cryo suit that woman is wearing, sir. But what does that-" Guardmaster Ricardo interrupted him and pointed to the cryo pod. It was leaking thick red liquid from the inner sleeping part itself and orange tendrils growing out of the chamber to the floor, pulsating and moving ever so often. It was a bloody mess.

From what his enhanced eyes could see, Guardmaster Ricardo easily made out the white printed numbers covered in blood, indicating a date when she was put to cryo sleep. It read: EMMA C. KRENNIC -

MARCH/27/22 CRYO NUMBER:2005. "Twenty-two?" Benji said. "As in the year 2022? You don't think, sir that. . ."

With a turn of his head, the guardmaster gazed down on this mysterious woman, this Emma Krennic. "So the stories are true. This must mean Earth did have the technological capability for cryo pods during the 21st century. I have only seen this kind of similar tech and designs in the Alvinor Empire, on their deep voyage starships. But in 2022?"

One question slowly poured after another into his mind, trying to piece together this newfound mystery that was unfolding in front of them. It is historically known by all humans, who study and read of course, that humanity during the 21st century did not have the technology to create cryo pods or have spaceships made for intergalactic space travel just yet, but was completely capable of making 50-foot tall mechs called Reapers, that were used and made sometime just before World War II and showed not only a momentous change in humanity's military but also in its technological potential afterward.

Benji, being the strict young holyguard he is, had to make sure this wasn't some Demonik trickery, since there were many battle accounts from troopers and holyguard stating that demons tend to warp whatever environment they are in at will if they wanted to. Even contorting certain animate or inanimate objects, making it seem that they're real but in reality. . .there was never anything there, to begin with. From hearing these reports, numerous modifications and upgrades have been installed by knowledge priests and Mutarei tech engineers, one of the main upgrades being the Anomaly Detector.

But to his surprise, it gave no anomalous energy reading except the organic tendrils growing out of it. Then Benji used his battle helm's built-in metal scanner to confirm if the elements used to make the cryo pod were in fact elements that were only on Ancient Earth. A green circle bleeped green, indicating that the alloys that the cryo pod was made of, are metals that were only found on Ancient Earth.

Finally, just to be sure, he needed to confirm this with his guardian program Serma. "Serma." Benji hailed. "Yes, Holyguard Benji?" Serma waited for his command. "Serma, the readings from both scanners I just used now, can you confirm them, just to be sure?" Serma, without hesitation in her voice, answered swiftly to the young holyguard. "Of course, Holyguard Benji. This would only take mere seconds." Benji can see his guardmaster carefully observing the cryo pod just once more, then looking at the woman he held in his arms.

"Who are you, Krennic?" Having no knowledge of her name, the mystery of the cryo pod, the unfathomable power that possesses at her fingertips. Guardmaster Ricardo could only look and ask internally to her. "Who are you?" Done with her calculations, Serma answered Benji. "I am done with my calculations, Holyguard Benji. Yes, your scanners do not deceive you. I have run them over countless times and have found that yes, the cryo pod you scanned dates to over 100 centuries in the past. Earth's past, to be precise, sir."

Guardmaster Ricardo felt the very ship itself shift from the stray plasma bolts impacting the hull outside. He could sense that Captain Zendaya was holding off twenty Cultist battleships, five of them created purely from the Demonik Realm, firing pure Demonik energy streams at the Omori's shields, causing devastating damage. The rest of the crew of the Omori, the Baultus troopers, naval pilots, and the engineers. He needed to hurry and make a decision.

Investigate or complete the mission? Wanted to investigate further but was pulled back into his duties as a Holyguard, ordered by Emperor Baultus himself to retrieve the special cargo at all costs and destroy anything or anyone that stood in his path. "Holyguad Benji." Benji's mind clicked to the sudden voice of his guardmaster, commanding and inspirational as ever.

"Yes, guardmaster?" Guardmaster Ricardo switched on his Heavenly Father blade, using the pure psychic energy he beamed on his magnificent holy weapon that only veteran holyguard can wield, turned to face the young holygaurd and said to him. "Contact the others. We're getting out of here." Following his guardmaster past the maze created by the stacked containers, the old corpses of the crew combined with dead cultists. Benji held the engineer to his chest, keeping the extreme momentum they have built since the finding of the cryo pod, Benji shouted to his guardmaster, asking him.

"Shall I pinpoint an extraction zone for Captain Zendaya, sir?!" Guardmaster Ricardo kept his speed slicing through blockades of Demonik cultists, shoulder-slamming a few of them to bits while protecting Emma Krennic at all times. "Negative!!" He yelled, holding a 9-foot-tall cultist in his pathway. "Tell Captain Zendaya to track my power armor, that way she can teleport us all in one go!! The demons will be expecting us to make an extraction zone! Tell her, Benji."

Benji switched his channels to the Omori and could see Captain Zendaya in the corner of the visor. Facing frustration, in the background numerous crew members scrambled to the different repair consoles, reacting to the energy bursts that busted panels off the walls. The sound of high-frequency rifles being fired off into unknown targets, Baltus troopers taking cover behind drop shields that have been deployed. "Captain Zendaya! Captain Zendaya, are you all right?!"

Grunting from a plasma bolt that nicked her right shoulder, incapacitating her for five seconds. Groaning, slamming her fist down, she raised her head high and yelled to the defending trooper behind her. "Cover me, fragdammit! Don't let those Demonik cultists get through!" She looked back to the viewscreen and leaned down into her chair, ensuring that her body was not exposed to stray plasma bolts this time. "Yes, Holyfuard Benji. What is it?"

From her belt, she pulled a synthetic healing spray, temporary but effective. Applying the spray to the burnt area, hissing as it did its magic. As she removed the charred part of her skinsuit, Benji continued. "Captain Zendaya! I have excellent news. We have found the special cargo. Woah!" He ran faster and faster, ramming multiple cultists over, his weight crushing them under his boots. "You found it! That's terrific news! Ahh, Emperors be praised. Alright, where's the extraction point, Benji?" He made a "no" gesture with his face.

"No, no! Guardmaster Ricardo has specifically ordered me to tell you not to pinpoint a certain area in the cargo bay as an extraction point. He said to track his power armor to pinpoint a location. After we're all regrouped, I'll give the all clear and you can use the jump to teleport us onto the Omori!" Captain Zendaya agreed, a small explosion happened about 20 feet away from her chair, troopers flinging into the air past her viewscreen.

"I got to go, Benji. May the Celestials bless you all!" Demons hung themselves from the containers and watched the speeding tanks run through the maze of containers, mapping it out as head nearer and nearer to other holyguard. "Amata, do you copy? Amata." Benji switched back to the local channel where it was only among his fellow holyguard.

"I hear you, Benji." Amata replied. "I hear you." Amata dodged two laser streams that almost hit her head and hardened her psychic shield. "Why, what happened?! Is the guardmaster alright?" She implored. "The guardmaster is fine, he just had to confirm something before we moved on. But yes, we have special cargo. We're getting ready to teleport back to the Omori. I honed in on your location and we're almost there-"

From her end, it sounded like he had to duck from some large blade that nearly cleaved off his head and continued to run. "Don't have time to deal with you demons! Ugh, be ready for us, we'll be coming in from the southern row section. Benji out!"

Laser beams deflected off her psychic shield pointlessly as she got the new orders from Benji, slowly gazing to the southern section, hearing Demonik cultists being clobbered and sliced in the distance. Ducking for cover, she butted the proton longshot on her thigh, took out the battery, and engaged the cooling systems for the automatic sniper rifle.

She could hear another Demonik cultist vigorously climb up the container wall with little effort, laughing and slobbering as he did. Gritting a blade between his teeth, he was shocked to find a bulky female holyguard waiting for him, smiling at his scared face. Eyes filled with fear, he half screamed and his head decapitated when Amata shouted *Sach*, which in Moderian tongue translated to "behead".

In a single action, one of her ancestral daggers came flying out of thin air, spinning so fast it was a blur to the eye. Hearing the body thud to the floor, she could help but take in a little joy once in a while. Due to her being half Moderian, which was known for their sadistic tendencies in battle, tried hard to resist the urge of taking great pleasure from the enemy's deaths. Being a trained holygaurd, she controlled her feelings and breathed deeply.

Waving her hand in retrieving motion, the dagger quickly came back to her side and vanished into thin air. Crouching back behind her previous cover, checking if the proton longshot was finished cooling down. The light lit green and the weapon beeped, indicating that it was ready for a new battery to be inserted. Continuous laser fire can be heard hitting the container walls, with an occasional plasma grenade to shake things up.

After taking this fortress that was beforehand by Demonik cultists, was now under the current guard by both Amata and Craig's watchful eyes. For over ten minutes, the two holyguard have taken a strong foothold here, holding off dozens of both Demonik cultists and demons together, attempting to climb over the container walls and kill them. Amata and Craig will not be so easily overturned by pawns of the Demonik, for despite their numbers, have secured this fortress front and back, ensuring it's safe for their fellow holyguard to return.

After casting two long prayers to Alsupra himself, Amata had felt comfort in knowing that both the guardmaster and Benji were alright, but something still clinging to her thoughts made her worry still. Looking out to the north rows of containers, stretching far and wide, she wondered about the condition of Holyguard Nepo. "Where are you, Nepo?"

She whispered under her lips, while on the opposite side where she was defending, Craig disconnected a plasma chaingun from its mounted position. Mowing down wave after pitiful wave of Demonik followers that dared showed themselves in her sights. Thick plasma bolts melted through both armor and the flesh, exiting out the back followed by strewn trails of leftover plasma, while some would even instantaneously become green goop.

Craig could see Amata keeping her side clear, firing consecutive shots from her proton longshot, then shouted to her. "Amata!" A laser stream passed Craig's head. "So what did Benji say? What're the orders?" Keeping behind cover, she replied swiftly to her fellow holyguard.

CHAPTER 12

Escape.

"GUARDMASTER RICARDO and Benji have found the special cargo! They're moving in on our location as we speak. They'll come from the northern side, behind us. Oh, also. . . the special cargo is human, too! The last name is Krennic, never heard of the name though. I searched through fifteen databases a while ago and have found nothing. Strange, don't you think?" Craig had eyes of confusion, followed by a nod of the head.

"Not focusing on that right now but I'll keep it noted! So, woah!" A demon with large feathery, long wings flapped above her and tried to snatch her by the shoulders, its sharp talons scraping against her psychic shield when it glided past. Unhooking her impact hammer she clipped on her belt, Craig mustered enough psychic energy to her weapon, making it three times more deadly. Targeting the demon, she threw the weapon so hard and fast at the feather-covered demon that when it hit, it exploded in a single gigantic poof.

The demon's body parts, feathers, and all came splattering all over the fortress. Amata continued her fire, taking out multiple Demonik cultists in mere seconds, until in the distance she could hear a familiar voice, from a fellow holyguard echoing among the annoying voices of the Demonik followers. Hearing containers being smashed through, going through each one of them, heading for the fortress. Amata could sense that it was. . .Nepo! "Nepo! Nepo, over here. We're over here!"

The last container he smashed through revealed his entire stature, groaning in pain and annoyed expression. He formed a concentrated energy barrier where it blocked most projectiles, his eyes scorched and bleeding, teeth-gritting from the burning sensation. But his face changed, his attention caught when he heard Amata's kind voice and a small smile grew.

Continuing to run in the direction of the fortress, not stopping for a single moment, clearing any dumb cultist who got in his way. "I hear you, Amata! I hear you! Watch out for me!" He jumped so high, above the three stacked containers, every ten feet in comparison to each other.

Desperate rotted hands and elongated claws reached out for him when leaped, some even throwing their weaponry and firing a mixture of laser bolts at him in mid-jump. None being successful, none gaining a grip on him. Whooshing past Amata's guard point on the container wall, landing down with precision that it would be impossible for someone with his injuries to land on the floor, properly and safely.

But holyguard enhancements allowed them to survive some of the harshest of battle scenarios that have been epic-sized, for better or for worse. But even with his sustained injuries, he landed perfectly, switching his ears in the directions and positions of his fellow holyguard, who from what he sensed, were doing their best to defend this fortress until Guardmaster and Benji arrived with the special cargo. In an attempt to rejoin his fellow holyguard in battle, his legs suddenly failed to support him.

Unable to get up from his kneed crouched position, with burnt eyes on his legs, feeling the energy from slowly being drained. "Tan, what's happening to my legs?" Scanning what physical damage has been done, to her surprise, nothing has happened to his lower bodily limbs. Scanning deeper and deeper, she found it was his power armor's leg servos that were completely busted, hydraulic liquid streaming slowly down his armored leg.

"Due to the extreme amount of damage inflicted to your power armor, especially those Demonik vexed grenades rounds, were able to melt through the durainium coating. Also, the regina in your eyes has suffered from an extremely high form of ultraviolet light, burning them out, literally bursting with fire. Thank Alsupra that you are still alive, Nepo!" Tan implored, with great worry in her voice.

But Nepo couldn't help, despite how serious his current condition was, feel comical in the pain he felt. Knowing that physical pain to a holyguard is temporary at all times. "Thank Alsupra indeed, Tan." Having sarcasm, he slowly lowered himself to the floor, letting out a soft cheerful laugh, laying down comfortably on his back.

"Thank Alsupra indeed. Ah, this hurts so much." He laid a hand across his chest, exhaling loudly, and could hear Craig jump down to where he was, kneeling, accessing his healing system, and inserting as carefully as she could a more potent painkiller into his nervous system, via the neck area.

Normally, this would take some time to get the holyguard back up on his feet but with her medical expertise, she could see that by the fourth-degree burns encircling his eyes and not critical damage to both retinas, she had to act fast and with haste. As the medical officer of her team and as a holyguard, Craig made this decision of her own will. Even though it went against most medical regulations in the Three Empires military, she had no choice but to use her experimental treatments.

Grabbing a tiny rectangular container on her utility belt, she paused and gazed at it. Unable to see anything but white rings encompassed in blackness, his head became fuzzier and fuzzier every second, barely being able to keep his head up anymore, he tried to tense his fingers but could feel nothing but numbness. Starting from his hands and then to his arms, soon his entire body succumbed to the unknown serum that Craig injected into his nervous system.

"That's new. . .that's. . .painkiller or some. . ." He tried to speak but his lips didn't follow, dizzying his conscious brain. The last thing he could hear just before he passed out was the sound of heavy footsteps darting into the fortress where he lay, recognizing the familiar patterns that made these footsteps were none other than his guardmaster and Benji, both who were carrying with them feminine humanoids. The last he heard was Benji's voice, out of breath and exhausted. "Now, captain. Recall us now!"

A laser bolt fired from a long ranged distance, depending on the model and the condition of the weapon, can do lethal damage to the body. Very lethal if the target is not wearing proper protection, either it being imorn ceramic plate armor or the more military-grade, crysamite armor. Fortunately for the captain, the uniform she wore had crysamite fibers sewn with the threads, making it mostly resistant to laser and high frequency, but impervious to any type of ballistics.

Her wound was freshly cauterized and bleeding, a minor irritation in the captain's ever-vigilant mind, taking cover behind the drop shields deployed by the troopers who came to her aid via the jump teleportation port nearby. Four of these troopers were veterans of the Baultus Empire, three being gunner sergeants and one a lieutenant.

The sergeants, armed with proton shotguns modded with a lighter cooling system and longer barrels, gave them a more long range of damage. Less spread, more compact, and to the point. The brown-colored crysamite armor reflected the energy projectiles that whizzed past, some laser bolts hitting their energy shields that fielded around their bodies. Looking like beautiful put-together glass when damaged.

They wore no helmets, revealing to Captain Zendaya that they must've got the word of the onboard threats and were probably either sleeping or training rookies beforehand. Recognizing the lieutenant when he unleashed his high-frequency chaingun upon the Demonik cultists, keeping a steady barrage. In the current situation, twelve Demonik cultists somehow teleported onto the Omori, specifically the bridge where Captain Zendaya commanded, without the use of jumpspace teleportation.

Making it impossible for Captain Zendaya to cancel any possible jump point entries via her wrist computer, which allowed her to activate any nearby jump teleporter or recall certain targets if needed. Ordering her guardian program to download the command console systems onto it, doing it just in time before it got destroyed by a lobbed plasma grenade.

Back against the drop shield itself, dropping an empty battery clip from her heavy pistol's grip and slid in a fresh, squarish barrel of the weapon. A small light flashed red to blue after she reloaded. Double checking, Captain Zendaya looked at the left side of the barrel, where the ammo counter was. It was a hundred, like the last one.

"This isn't good." Sighing discomforts. "My shots mean nothing to their Demonik armor!" To her right, the scarred Sgt shouted to her, still shooting. "Captain, they're not going to stop until they have that wrist computer! Ow!" Plasma enveloped the top portion of his energy shield, immediately taking cover, groaning with frustration. "Or until you're dead! No offense."

Smiling, understanding the trooper's words. "None taken! Since they also created the two jumpspace ports in the bridge, reinforcements won't show up for another fifteen minutes. The other troopers are probably dealing with whatever got aboard my Omori!" The second Sgt to her left, his proton shotgun out of ammo, called to both troopers for covering fire.

"We don't have fifteen minutes, captain. We need the holyguard." He said, inserting battery slugs into his proton shotgun's slot. "Once they give the word and have the special cargo, I can manually recall them directly into the bridge with us, letting them take care of the rest." Popping out of cover briefly, she fired her heavy pistol, hitting two Demonik cultists in their chests, each being sent flying backward from the compact energy projectile. Black blood could be seen oozing out of the fallen corpses, choking and twitching.

She ducked down behind the drop shield, taking more and more damage from the plasma bolt onslaught the cultists were giving. Her wrist computer made a beeping noise, showing Holygurd Benji was trying to speak through the com channel. Not sparing a single moment, she pressed a button and the voice channel flicked on. "Now, captain. Recall us now!"

Eyes widened, praying to Alsupra that they have finally got the special cargo, half relieved and terrified. Swiping her wrist computer's screen with haste, scrolling down the command console's many primary ship systems, finding one marked as "Jumpspace/recall: pinpoint: guardmaster.". No hesitation at heart, she pressed the holographic key, recalling the guardmaster, along with the rest of his team back aboard the Omori, the bridge.

Where Captain Zendaya, along with the three troopers were defending at all costs. Four blue large pillars, golden rings of light encircling them, formed suddenly in front of the drop shield, for some reason it seemed like he was laying down. Captain Zendaya gasped. Was one of them injured, she thought? Was Guardmaster Ricardo alright? And she just recalled at the worst possible moment even if they were all injured.

To her relief and many prayers, the first one appearing was none other than the guardmaster, who was carrying a human woman in his arms, most likely the special cargo dubbed by Emperor Baultus himself. When he appeared, the firing from both sides stopped, the Demonik cultists showing fear explicitly plain. Rejoice at his arrival, Captain Zendaya was appalled with tears in her eyes. "Guardmaster! You're alive!" His body was severely damaged, his power armor wrecked and his helmet gone, Guardmaster Ricardo was happy that he and his team got out alive. Sighing slowly, he replied to the captain.

"Yes. Yes, I am." A stupidly brave Demonik cultist, girded his loins and approached, scoffing at his presence. "Pfft! Holyguard scum! Do not think that you-" Pop! Every cultist blew up into solid iron nuggets bouncing off the metal floor, covered in black blood. "Hmm, they were all human after all."

Guardmaster Ricardo smirked, not turning once behind him, and called to the trooper near Captain Zendaya. "Lieutenant. Please take this woman, she needs immediate medical attention." Running to the towering guardmaster, he gently took her and carried her away, his path leading him to the gravlift. Pass the iron nuggets and blood-covered weapons scattered across the floor, glancing at the sight, shrugging his shoulders in an astounded manner.

The remaining troopers left Captain Zendaya's side to secure the bridge and made doubly sure that there was no Demonik cultist or even worse demons alive. Holstering her heavy pistol, retightening her combat belt, running her gloved hands through her hair, and walking to the guardmaster with speed. "How badly are you hurt, Ricardo?" Hugging him tightly, trying her best to encompass him with her arms. His reaction to her doing this, as a holyguard but mostly as a friend, gave a warm smile.

"Extremely." He wheezed, collapsing to a kneeling position, catching in his hand blood he coughed up from the internal wounds. "Ricardo! Your power armor's healing systems-" Nodding slowly, he interrupted her. "Yes, yes. Holyguard Craig had told me already." Turning around to see three of his holyguard appear, Craig, attending to an unconscious Nepo and Amata with a demon's head in her grasp, with a confused look on her face, searching for someone.

Sensing something off deeply, he scanned the entire room, searching for . . . "Captain." Captain Zendaya could see his face stricken with fear. "Where's Benji?" To her realization also, Holyguard Benji was nowhere to be seen. Scrambling through her wrist computer's different command systems, pressing the jumpspace tab. She needed to think fast, but couldn't concentrate due to her wound. "Callis, scan for any interferences on the holyguard's jumpspace recall to the Omori. Please make haste!" She waited, her heart rate rising with every pace she took.

"Captain." Callis said. "Yes, what have you found?" She implored. "On the holyguard's return to the Omori, Holyguard Benji's jump recall was interfered by an unknown energy force, unlike anything I have encountered before. I tried to trace the point of origin, but so far I can't confirm anything except one thing." Her mouth agape from this answer, she asked. "What interfered with his recall?" Captain Zendaya asked Callis. "Not what, captain. . .but who?"

"Where am I?" Benji did a 360 spin, scanning his mysterious new surroundings, and holding the engineer in his arms. "Captain Zendaya, do you copy? Something must've happened during mid-recall. Captain, are you there?" Nothing but silence on his com channel, an eerie silence. He increased his psychic shields tenfold, ensuring both of their safety.

From what his eyes could see, a black night starry sky, purple clouds overpassing and the trees. . .the tree's trunks were completely burnt to the core, leaving only ghostly, skeletal versions of what they once were. There wasn't even a gentle breeze. Branches uncannily still attached, he switched to the ground that he stood on.

The dirt itself, from what his helmet's visor scanned, was no longer fertile to support any form of plant life. "What happened to this planet?" His psychic sense suddenly spiked when an eerie, uncanny yet familiar dark figure approached him out of the darkness behind him. His heart dropped, his body partially paralyzed from the immense psychic pressure that was being pushed down upon his soul. This was all caused by the dark figure who walked closer and closer to Benji.

For the first time in his life, he felt fear strike him like lightning from this unknown dark being, whose very presence was so powerful, that it even dwarfed Benji's powers by default. But he had to face this newfound threat, no matter how inconceivably powerful it was.

He gazed at the engineer. Praying hard to Alsupra to protect both their lives and survive, he slowly turned and stared into the deep abyssal eyes of the dark figure. Shocked by the appearance of the figure, Benji. . .gasped with widened eyes. Only silence and darkness followed after. . .

Note From The Author

Now that you've reached the end of this book, please know that I enjoyed writing every last bit from the intro to the conclusion/cliffhanger. What do you think will happen to Benji and the engineer girl? Why is Emma Krennic still alive? Can the Omori escape the Demonik battleships? Hopefully, more to come in the future, along with other short story projects too. I am Haviti Washington, a young writer inspired by many astounding works of fiction and fantasy. Thank you so much for taking the time to read!

As a reminder, this is a giant *introduction* to the GalaxyStar universe as a whole, setting the groundwork for most readers just getting started or into this both vast, expansive, mysterious, and epic universe. Technically, this shouldn't be the first entry to the universe due to the original story being about a son of a space pirate, traveling the Three Empires with his trusty second mate and a sprinkled crew of bad##ses! (Capable of killing Jedi if needed) Down below are my other book titles online that you can read! I hope you enjoy them as much as I had fun writing them!

2896: The Interplanetary War: The Capturing of General Philkus

2896: The Interplanetary War: TYPHON

Arcemo: Tales From The World Of Herta 1

If you are interested, please tell me which universe you would like to see first or more of! So long, farewell, and may the Celestials be forever with you in the journeys you make in life!

EXTRA BIT OF LORE IN the Galaxystar universe

In the year 12022, there are no clear explanations as to why the earth exploded or how it got to this point in the first place. Some theories hold that the Earth itself has suffered so much that, despite human attempts to fully heal it, it has drastically reduced its lifespan. Could it be the residual contamination of 2019 or perhaps even the mysterious 10,000 Year War? With limited resources, humans that were fortunate enough to leave Earth's destruction in time, boarded 4 giant spaceships built in the early years of spaceflight, humanity searched for other planets suitable for life in the solar system and most importantly, to live on.

Unfortunately, most of the other planets in the solar system showed signs of R.P.D(Rapid Planet Decay), making once habitable planets turn. . .uninhabitable. Soon after, they left their local solar system and continued their search for a temporary world to call home. Planet after planet after planet, there was nothing. But when mankind slowly started to lose faith in finding anything worth living for, a glimmer of hope shined upon them. This glimmer was the Celestials, a hyperintelligent alien race that existed before humans were even created, saw them and took pity on them. With their help, mankind created a device capable of making portals, channeling endless energy, and obtaining speeds faster than the speed of light itself. A combination of Earth's brilliant minds and the Celestials, they made the first jumpdrives. With the newly built jumpdrives, they traveled to nearby galaxies and introduced themselves to the plethora of alien races, some questioning the human's presence, while others honored them as if they were royalty or chosen by the Celestials. Throughout the beginning years, mankind gained power and grew quickly from galaxy to galaxy, slowly gaining control over the majority of the planets, through peace, the Celestial's influence, and of course, jumpdrive technology.

www.ingramcontent.com/pod-product-compliance
Ingram Content Group UK Ltd.
Pitfield, Milton Keynes, MK11 3LW, UK
UKHW021657190726
13853UKWH00001B/319